BOOK OF NO 4LEEP

無眠書4

2020年美國列出「全球最大生活壓力城市」排名，香港「榮獲」第一名；2022年另一個全球健康指數調查，香港的身心健康指數同樣拿到第一名，不過是倒數第一名，更是連續第三年於亞太地區位列榜末，實在是當之無愧。雖然調查已不是新鮮出爐，但仍然有一定的參考價值。

此外，近年香港的犯罪率有增長趨勢，有報導指2023年第一季的罪案數字較2022年同期激增48%。持刀傷人案更是屢見不鮮，幾乎隔幾天又有一單，被網民戲稱香港是個「國際大刀會」。而2023年2月轟動全港的「蔡天鳳碎屍案」，當中的犯案手法、牽涉人物、各種輿論，比電視劇、電影更離奇更駭人。

在香港這個非常高壓的地方，生活步伐急促，工時長假期少，而且地少人多，就連到離島遊玩也人頭湧湧，無法好好放鬆心情。種種因素堆疊起來，就變成了壓力和精神狀態轉差的催化劑，面對每天發生層出不窮的荒誕事情，要維持正常真的不容易。想到這裡我卻忽發奇想，萌生了今集的主題——瘋誕夜。

其實不只是香港，世界各地每天也越來越多令人費解的事，例如：俄羅斯堅稱是烏克蘭先動兵，及後俄羅斯「反擊」對住宅進行空襲，仍然否認針對民居攻擊；或是Netflix把埃及妖后寫成黑人，結果引起埃及人熱烈反抗，指 Netflix 企圖篡改歷史。當然，這兩件事只是冰山一角。而這些怎樣看也不合邏輯、看了就會很憤怒的事，卻有很多支持者擁護，這才是最可怕。

說了這麼多，無非都是想帶出，不論《No Sleep》系列的故事再怎麼陰森可怖，最瘋癲、最恐怖的始終還是現實。好吧，現在就帶你進入這個看似離譜卻又有點熟悉的瘋癲世界。

（題外話，今年還有另一件大事——AI 機械人逐漸普及化，當中最熱門的一定要提 ChatGPT。我還真的試過找它翻譯，幸好還未能取代真人翻譯，但再過幾年就很難說了，可能我的飯碗要丟了。或許某一天 AI 會成為主流，甚至反過來領導人類，誰知道呢？）

譯者

陳婉婷

CONTENTS
目錄

醉生夢死 Intoxicated Delusion

異想天開　Mind Boggling

Scorpion-Hearted
蛇蠍心腸

A Mother's Love Endures Through All

As the man grabbed my hand and led me away, my mother could no longer hold in her tears. She fell to the barren ground in front of him and began wailing.

"Please, please take me instead!" She sputtered through her sobs, "Please, I'll do anything!"

Tears cut streaks through her dirty face as she looked up at the man, pleading. "I'll do anything." She repeated.

The man glared at her, clearly disgusted, and continued to lead me away. I glanced behind my shoulder, getting one last glimpse of the woman who raised me. She burst into a new fit of desperate shrieks, face beet red and reaching out towards us.

"Please, she doesn't deserve this! She doesn't deserve this! Take me instead! Please!"

She continued howling on the ground behind us, but the man kept dragging me away.

He patted my back for comfort and said "Don't worry sweetheart, everything is going to be fine. We're trying to prioritize the children. There's only so much room in the bunker."

母愛偉大

那個男人拉著我的手帶我離開時，媽媽的淚水再也忍不住了。她跌坐在男人面前那片光禿禿的地上，嚎啕大哭起來。

「拜託，帶走我吧，不要帶走她！」她抽泣著說：「求求你，我甚麼都願意做！」

淚水劃過她骯髒的臉龐，她抬頭向男人懇求著，並重複道：「我任勞任怨。」

男人厭惡地瞪了瞪媽媽，繼續把我帶走。我回頭瞥了一眼，看了看這個把我撫養成人的女子最後一眼。她絕望得撕心裂肺地尖叫起來，叫得滿臉通紅，伸手想抓向我們。

「拜託，不可以讓這些事發生在她身上！她不該受這樣的對待！讓我來代替她吧！求求你！」

男人無視在我們身後地上嚎叫不斷的媽媽，繼續拖著我離開。

他拍拍我的背，安慰著說：「親愛的，別擔心，一切都會好起來的。我們會優先帶走孩子，畢竟地堡裡的空間就只有這麼大。」

Chris Never Hit Me

Chris never hit me, mum. I want to make that clear. I know it's tough to plan a funeral, I know you'll have a million questions. You and dad have been crying all night and I don't think it'll ever end. You scream questions into the emptiness, not realising I can hear them. You ask me why, but Chris never hit me, and I was in love. I thought it would be okay. I didn't know it would end this way.

Chris never hit me. When we moved in together last year, in that neighbourhood that was far too traditional, everything was perfect. We showered each other with gifts and love. After a long day at work cleaning, hands calloused from the harsh chemicals, I'd come home to rose petals and a long bath.

Chris never hit me. I know you thought I could do better than a plumber. You wanted me to find someone wealthy, to never worry about money like you did, but we managed. Sure things were stressful at times. Sometimes we would shout, but what couples don't argue from time to time?

Chris never hit me. Sometimes the stress would get too much. Sometimes tempers would be lost, harsh words exchanged, but then the gifts would come back and I'd remember how loved I was. Everyone makes mistakes, surely it's okay as long as they're sorry? Favourite meals and apologies. I could see their guilt. I knew it wouldn't happen again.

Chris 從不打我

媽媽，Chris 從來都沒有打過我。我想要釐清這件事。我知道籌備葬禮很煩惱，我知道你們有成千上萬的疑問。你和爸爸整晚都在哭，看來這個情境永遠不會結束。你們對著空氣大聲問的問題，其實我都聽到了。你問我為甚麼，但 Chris 從不打我，而且我眼裡只有愛情。我以為會沒事的，也沒想過事情會以這種方式結束。

Chris 從不打我。去年我們搬到那個極度傳統的社區同居，一切都很完美。我們會用禮物和愛沐浴對方。經過一整天的清潔工作後，我的雙手因長期接觸刺激性化學物質而長滿繭，但回到家就會看見玫瑰，又可以盡情泡浴。

Chris 從不打我。我知道你覺得我可以做其他比水電工更好的工作。你想我找個有錢人，那就不用像你一樣為錢發愁，但我們還是可以生活下去。當然，有時我們會壓力很大，會大吵大鬧，但情侶之間又有誰不吵架的呢？

Chris 從不打我。雖然有時壓力太大，會發脾氣，會互相説些難聽的話，但隨後又會有彌補的禮物，提醒我 Chris 有多愛我。每個人都會犯錯，只要他們感到抱歉就沒問題了吧？送上我最愛的食物和道歉就能獲得我的原諒。我看得出他們的罪惡感，而我知道這些錯事不會再發生了。

Chris never hit me. I did think about leaving once or twice. When I spilt that drink, and the glass went flying past my head. When the yelling went from minutes to hours. But it didn't happen too often, and the rest of the time everything was just so perfect. I just needed to be more careful, I'm just so clumsy. I just needed to get it right, then there would be no reason for yelling.

Chris never hit me, but I decided to leave anyway, not that you would know that. I put my foot down. Enough was enough. I wanted to feel safe. It hurt to throw away a year of my life, but I couldn't raise a family like this. But Chris was so mad, tried to talk me out of it.

Chris never hit me. It was an accident, I swear. I'm so clumsy. Chris was trying to stop me leaving and I was just trying to get out. I slipped and my elbow caught an eye. A black eye was rapidly forming. Chris was so mad, like I've never seen before. Stormed out before I could stop them.

Chris never hit me. But I heard her voice from the other room loud and clear, squeaking slightly from the anger. "Help, my boyfriend is attacking me!"

Chris 從不打我。我的確有一兩次想過要離開。那次我灑了那杯飲料，玻璃杯就從我頭上飛過。大吵大鬧由幾分鐘變成持續幾小時。但這些情況並不常發生，其餘時間一切都很完美。我只需要更加小心，我太笨拙了。我只需要把事情做好，就沒有的大喊大叫理由了。

Chris 從不打我。但我還是決定離開，悄悄地離開。我已經立定決心，我忍夠了。我想要安全感。浪費了一年的光陰很可惜，但我無法再這樣養家下去。但是 Chris 非常生氣，想說服我放棄這個念頭。

Chris 從不打我。我發誓那次只是意外，因為我很笨拙。Chris 想阻止我離開，但我想出去。我滑倒了，手肘撞到了Chris 的眼睛，瞬間就瘀成一片。Chris 前所未有地暴怒起來，我完全無法制止。

Chris 從不打我。但我聽見她響亮而清晰、因憤怒帶點嘶啞的聲音，從另一個房間傳出：「救命啊，我男朋友打我！」

Chris never hit me, but as the police stormed down the door, in that far too traditional neighbourhood, I finally realised the truth.

Chris didn't need to hit me.

Chris 從不打我。可是，身處那個極度傳統的社區，警察破門衝進來時，我終於明白了真相。

Chris 根本不需要打我。

"This is Your Captain Speaking..."

I'd opted for the cheap red-eye flight home from Houston to Toronto. I could have taken the morning flight, but I was anxious to get home. I don't think my wife was happy that my business trips had restarted post-pandemic.

I was at the front of the plane, and had a clear view of the cockpit door. I could remember going in there as a kid, the pilots showing me the buttons. They definitely don't do that anymore. I heard somewhere that now the doors are locked for the whole flight.

We were an hour or so into the flight, most of the passengers were sleeping or had headphones in, oblivious to the world around them. I was reading when I heard a shout followed by a muffled thump coming from the cockpit.

Startled, A nearby flight attendant tapped on the door and asked if everything was alright. The silence must have unnerved her, because she whispered something into the intercom next to her. Two more attendants arrived from the back of the plane and she drew the curtain closed behind them. More knocks and murmurs came from behind the curtain. Nervously, I put down my book and watched.

Suddenly the intercom boomed to life, shaking most from their sleep and making me jump.

「以下是機長廣播。」

我選擇了從侯斯敦到多倫多的廉價通宵航班回家。我本可以乘坐早上的航班，但我歸心似箭。疫情後我回復出差，我老婆對此並不高興。

我坐在飛機的前頭，可以看到駕駛艙門。我記得小時候進過裡面，機師示範不同按鈕給我看。他們現在絕對不會再這樣做了。我聽說現在整個飛行過程中，駕駛艙門都會是鎖著的。

我們飛行了一個小時左右，大多數乘客都在睡覺或戴著耳機，彷彿與世隔絕。我在看書的時候，聽見駕駛艙裡有人喊叫了一聲，然後「砰」的一聲悶響。

附近的一名乘務員受驚地走上前敲了敲門，詢問是否一切安好。沉默應該使她很不安，因為她對著旁邊的對講機低聲說了些甚麼。又有兩名乘務員從機尾方向趕來，然後拉上了他們身後的簾子。更多的敲門聲和呢喃聲從窗簾後面傳來。我緊張得放下書觀望。

突然間，廣播大聲響了起來，把大部分乘客從睡夢中吵醒，我也嚇得跳了起來。

"Good evening folks! This is your Captain, Lawrence Andrews, speaking. I hope everyone is having a marvelous flight here on Zip! Airlines. Usually my co-captain Eric handles the announcements, but he's unable to come to the intercom, so I'll be handling both tonight! We're currently cruising at 30,000 ft and what a beautiful night it is!"

I could see everyone moving from irritation to nervousness. Something was wrong, the Captain's voice sounded *off*. He was out of breath and his enthusiasm seemed fake. I heard the attendants knock again as the Captain continued speaking.

"Folks, as a company, Zip! Airlines know their customers are the most discount-oriented people around. That's why we offer the cheapest rates of any airline in North America!"

I'd stood up at this point, along with a few others. People were looking around uncertainly. The Captain started again, his voice rising to a shout, "And have any of you stopped to consider HOW we keep these rates so low? Well folks, we do that by squeezing our employees for all we can. Long shifts, no raises, even pay cuts! All so you a**holes can fly in a JET PLANE for under $300!"

「各位晚安！我是你們的機長 Lawrence Andrews。希望各位在活力航空會有一段美妙旅程。通常是副機長 Eric 進行廣播，但他現在無法過來使用廣播系統，所以今晚我會一人處理這兩個事項！我們目前正在三萬呎的高空巡航，這是個多麼美麗的夜晚啊！」

聽罷每個人的心情都由煩躁變成緊張。有些不妥，船長的聲音不太*對勁*。他氣喘吁吁，而且表達出現的熱情很虛偽。機長繼續說話時，我聽到乘務員再次敲門。

「各位，作為一家公司，活力航空非常了解我們的客戶最注重就是優惠。這就是為甚麼我們在所有北美航空公司是最便宜的！」

我頓時站了起來，有其他幾個人也站了起來。人們不安地環顧四周。機長又開口了，把聲線提高到喊叫的程度：「你們有沒有人停下來想過我們是如何將價格保持如此之低？各位，是通過不斷壓榨我們的員工來達成目的。工時長，沒有加薪，甚至減薪！這一切都是為了讓你們這些混蛋不用三百美元就能乘坐噴射機！」

A few men had come to the front of the plane. It sounded like they were trying to break down the cockpit door. Panic bubbled up into a sob in my chest and I wished I could call my wife.

The Captain was back again, sounding resolute.

"To those of you who expect everything for nothing, to those who expect people to slave away for your profits, f**k every last one of you. Please consider this my resignation."

A collective shriek tore through the plane as the nose began to dip forward.

有好幾個男人來到了飛機的前頭，聽起來他們似乎正試圖打破駕駛艙門。恐慌在我胸膛翻滾，然後演變成啜泣。我真希望能打電話給我老婆。

機長的聲音又響起了，聽起來很堅決。

「那些希望不勞而獲的人，那些期望他人為你自己的利益而奴役的人，聽好了，你們每個人都去死吧。這就當是我的辭職信。」

機頭向下傾斜時，尖叫聲劃破機艙。

Jealousy Really Does Bring Out The Worst in People

I know that people are jealous of me. How can they not be?

I date fantastic men. My last conquest was a gorgeous man; olive skin and long eyelashes. He had the best taste in clothing and bought me expensive jewelry. I loved the luxurious sheets on his bed. It's a damn shame — he and I could have made a powerful couple. But at the end of the day, he couldn't handle me.

I have a terrific job. Sure, everyone I work with is an imbecile; I'm used to that, though. It's just something that happens to be a lot less… controversial than my side projects. I work with potent neurotoxins, testing the threshold for lethality, symptoms at various stages of exposure, whether antidotes exist… ya know, your usual "for the betterment of human life" spiel. It's all bullsh*t. It's not my job to improve other people's lives. It's not my fault that they're jealous of mine.

I own some pretty nice things. The latest iPhone? Got it. The best noise-cancelling headphones on the market? Got'em. The classic cars? Well, I DO have them — they're just tucked away. A fleet of old-school classic cars outside of my sh*tty apartment building would draw too much attention. Attention means producing the paperwork and explaining how they came to be mine. And explanations like that just create more work for me.

妒能害賢

我知道人們妒忌我。他們怎麼可能不妒忌嘛？

我都跟優秀的男人約會。我上一個征服的是個擁有橄欖色肌膚及纖長睫毛的帥哥。他有著頂級的服裝品味，還給我買了昂貴的珠寶。我很喜歡他鋪在床上的那些豪華床單。真是太可惜了——他和我本可以成為一對厲害的夫妻，但最終，他應付不了我。

我有一份很棒的工作。當然，和我一起工作的每個人都是低能兒；不過我已經習慣了。我的工作只是碰巧比我的業餘項目沒那麼……有爭議性。我與強效神經毒素打交道、測試致死的臨界值、不同劑量的症狀、有沒有解毒劑……那些嘩眾取寵的甚麼「為了改善人類生活」，全都是廢話。改善別人的生活不是我的工作。他們嫉妒我也不是我的錯。

我擁有很多好東西：最新款的 iPhone？有啦。市面上最好的降噪耳機？也有啦。老爺車？唔，我確實也有——只是藏起來了。在我破爛的公寓樓下停著整排老爺車太過招搖了。要是引起了注意，就會意味著要處理文書工作，解釋我如何獲得它們，而像這樣的解釋只會令我要處理更多事務。

I came up from nothing; married young to a useless drunk, had to watch him waste away as he spent all of my money on whiskey and cigarettes. His memory was the first thing to go. It was fascinating. The man I married may have been selfish, but he wasn't stupid. I could never stand to have a partner of lesser intellect. To see his brain turn to mush as it floated in a puddle of whiskey was the beginning of my research.

Alcohol, you see, is a neurotoxin. Lead is another. Mercury. Car exhaust. Certain insecticides. And my own creation. My little side projects.

With the right dose, you can make a man forget who he is, what he owns, even how you met.

A small exposure will distract you when a little cash goes missing from your sock drawer.

A stronger dose will make you just so, so adorably suggestible and easy to control.

And a large dose — well, if circulated through the vent system for maximum distribution in every room of the house, a large dose can turn a PhD into a stuttering, drooling, mindless old man.

我「白手興家」——年輕時嫁給了一個沒用的酒鬼，眼睜睜看著他日漸消瘦，因為他把我所有錢都花在了威士忌和香煙上。最先消失的是他的記憶，真有趣。我嫁的這個男人可能很自私，但他並不愚蠢。我無法忍受有一個智力較低的伙伴。看著他的腦袋漂浮在一灘威士忌中漸漸變成糊狀，啟發了我進行研究。

看吧，酒精是一種神經毒素。鉛也是，還有水銀、汽車廢氣、某些殺蟲劑。還有我自己的創作，那些小小的業餘項目。

如果劑量適中，你可以讓一個人忘記他是誰、他擁有甚麼，甚至忘記你們是如何認識的。

小劑量會讓你注意不到襪子抽屜裡少了一點現金。

中劑量會讓你變得耳根軟，易於控制。

大劑量的話——如果透過通風系統使它盡可能地散落在屋裡每個房間，大劑量可以讓一個博士生變成一個口吃、流口水、失智的老人。

And then I find a new one. I show off what I've gained. And the cycle repeats.

I don't care about the dirty looks. The accusing glares from their families. The former friends of mine who made a few connections — nothing a little man-made amnesia won't cure.

And why should I care?

I know they're just jealous of me.

然後我就去找新目標，再炫耀我的收穫，週而復始。

我不在乎他們家人那些厭惡的臉色或是指責的目光。要是我以前的朋友們發現了甚麼蛛絲螞跡——人為的失憶症都能「治癒」它們。

但又關我甚麼事？

我知道他們只是妒忌我。

Ouch!

Ouch. What the hell?

He felt a sharp, stabbing pain in his side. He hadn't hit anything, though. In fact, he was just standing there, making a PB&J[1], when it happened.

After the flare subsided, he went back to his sandwich, filing the weird jab away into "random body aches" in his mind.

Huh.

Ouch! Again? Maybe I should go to the doctor.

Another pain, maybe an hour later, similar to the first but stronger in intensity and longer in duration before it faded. It had also migrated from his side to right under his rib cage.

He called and made an appointment for the next day, and resumed his day.

---

1 PB&J : Peanut Butter & Jam

哎呦！

哎呦。搞甚麼鬼？

他感到身側傳來一陣劇烈的刺痛。但明明他沒有撞倒甚麼東西。他只是站在那裡，弄著花生醬果醬三文治，刺痛就突然閃現。

痛楚平息後，他邊吃著三文治，邊把這個奇怪的刺痛記在腦海裡，歸類為「無緣無故的身體疼痛」。

唉。

哎呦！又來？或者我應該去看看醫生。

又一陣刺痛，大概只隔了一個小時。與初次那陣刺痛差不多，但痛感更強，持續了更久才消失。這次疼痛由身側移至肋骨下方。

他打電話預約了明天去看醫生，然後繼續幹活。

OUCH! Holy f**k!

This time, the pain was within his left ribs, and it occurred less than half an hour after the earlier one. It took his breath away for a solid few seconds, and it was all he could do to keep from crying out.

He pulled his hand away, and saw a slow bloom of red dot on his grey shirt.

I'm bleeding? How?

Something was wrong, he knew it now. But what, he didn't know.

He looked at the clock. Nearly five.

Kara will be home soon. I need to get to the hospital.

Agh…!

10 minutes later, the "phantom" pain returned, no longer intangible. He could feel the blood leaking from his heart; it felt like a hole had been punched through him.

哎呦！！他媽的！

這一次，刺痛在他的左肋骨裡爆發，距離上次疼痛不到半小時。這次讓他足足有好幾秒鐘無法呼吸，他強忍著不讓自己大叫起來。

他拿開本來掩住肋骨的手，竟然看見灰色襯衫上慢慢綻放出一個紅點。

我在流血？搞甚麼？

他知道自己有些不妥，但到底是甚麼不妥，他不知道。

他看了看鐘，將近五點。

Kara 很快就會回家了，我要去醫院。

啊⋯⋯！

十分鐘後，「幻痛」又再來襲，而且不再是無形的。他感覺到鮮血從他的心臟流出，就像有人在他身上打了一個洞。

The door opened.

Kara!

She stared down at her boyfriend, collapsed on the ground, and was so shocked she dropped the contents of her hands onto the floor beside him.

"You're not-" she started.

"Help…" he pleaded, as his eyes turned to what she'd dropped.

A lump of warm, brown clay, wrapped in a ribbon and impaled by a long sewing needle.

His rapidly-fogging mind could barely make sense of the sight, and he had three thoughts before he couldn't think anymore.

Why?
Looks more like a potato than a doll.
Maybe that's why she had trouble finding the heart…

And the clay doll grew cold as he faded away.

門打開了。

Kara！

Kara 低頭望著倒在地上的男朋友，震驚得把手上的物品丟在他身旁的地板上。

「你不是——」Kara 先開口。

「救我……」他懇求道，目光轉向那些掉落在地上的東西。

一團溫暖的棕色黏土，上面包裹著一條絲帶，一根長長的縫衣針刺穿了黏土。

他瞬間意識模糊，不能理解眼前的景象，在他無法思考之前，冒出了三個念頭：

為甚麼？
看起來像個馬鈴薯而不是像隻娃娃。
也許這就是她找不到心臟的原因……

黏土娃娃變冷了，他逝去了。

AITA for
Not Helping the "Other Woman"?

Throwaway for obvious reasons.

I have been with my boyfriend "John" (fake name) for the past 2 years, and we've lived together for the last year. I do try to trust him, but I've caught him a few times talking to other women so my trust is a little limited I admit. He's sworn he would never do it again though, I believed him until recently.

The problem is "Anna" (also a fake name). Anna has been with us for the last 6 months, and she has always been a pain in the ass for me, to be honest I hate her. She's always complaining and is loud enough to keep us up at night. She cries if we refuse to help her with anything. I feel like she's manipulating us whenever she wants food or anything else that she's just too lazy to get, but John always gets her what she wants. I want her to go but John is always saying we can't do that, she needs us, she has nowhere else to go. All that standard stuff.

I thought he was just being nice to her, but now I'm not so sure. He's talking to her a lot, and spending a lot of time with her. He has started staying up late in her room. I caught him cuddling with her last night. I once thought I heard him say he loves her! He denies anything is happening and calls me crazy, but I know that I'm not.

對第三者見死不救的壞妻子

這是個分身帳號。

我和男朋友 John（化名）交往已經兩年，去年我們同居了。我真的很想相信他，但我揭發過他幾次和其他女人說話，所以我承認其實我不太信任他。John 向我發誓他再也不會這樣做，我選擇了相信，直到最近發生了一些事。

問題出在 Anna（也是化名）身上。在過去的六個月，Anna 一直和我和 John 在一起。Anna 是個煩人的傢伙，看著她就覺得礙眼。老實說，我很討厭她。她總是在抱怨，聲音大得讓我們徹夜難眠。如果我們拒絕幫助她，她就會哭。我覺得每當她想要吃東西時，或是其他只是她懶得去做的事，她就會操縱我們，但 John 總是會滿足她的需求。我想趕她走，但 John 總是說我們不能這樣做，說 Anna 需要我們、她沒有容身之所，諸如此類的那些典型藉口。

我最初以為 John 只是出於禮貌地對她好，但現在我有些懷疑了。他經常和 Anna 說話，花很多時間陪她，而且開始在她的房間待得很晚。昨晚我還發現 John 抱著她。我有一次好像聽到 John 說他愛她！他否認所有事，更說我瘋了，但我知道我很正常。

I tried talking to her, but she just cried more. John and I had a big fight about this last night, and I've made some decisions. The first is that I need some space from John to feel more sane, so he's agreed to move back with his dad for a few weeks to save the relationship. The other is that I am making it clear to Anna that I won't be helping her any more. I'm not doing anything for her. It doesn't matter how much she cries. I can hear her crying in her room now, but she's not manipulating me anymore.

I think it's better to deal with this before she learns how to talk. AITA[1]?

Author: EJ Packham

---

1 AITA : Am I the a**hole?

我試著和 Anna 說話，但她只是哭得更慘。John 和我昨晚為此大吵了一架，而我做了一些決定。首先是我需要跟 John 分開一下，好讓我能理智一點。他同意搬回去和爸爸一起住個幾週，以挽救這段關係。另一件事是我向 Anna 明確表示我不會再幫助她了。就算她哭得有多慘，我也不會為她做任何事。我聽見 Anna 現在在自己的房間裡哭，但我不會再被她操縱了。

我認為最好在她學會說話之前解決這個問題。我是不是太壞了？

I Just Found Out that My Boyfriend Has Been Cheating on Me...

My boyfriend, Daniel, and I have been together for a few years. Despite our age difference, we get along extremely well and love each other very much. Daniel is the sweetest person I've ever met and I truly believe that he has helped build me into a better person. I never doubted his love and loyalty to me... However, today I found out he was cheating on me.

My suspicions started about three weeks ago. While showering, I found something in the drain that definitely DID NOT belong to me or Daniel.

I started bawling and immediately ran out to confront him. Even when waving the damn thing in front of his face, he didn't flinch at all. He was completely dismissive! He casually brushed off my concerns and left the room.

After that incident, I noticed how Daniel started to look disheveled at times. He's a very tidy, well put-together man, you see, so this was completely out of the ordinary. At that point, I was sure that he was fooling around with another woman. The worst part is... he started smelling like her too!

Every time I confronted him, he would change the subject or simply stare at me sternly. This terrible change in his behavior was tearing me apart.

男友出軌了

我和男朋友 Daniel 已經交往好幾年了。儘管有年齡差距，我們仍然相處融洽，互相深愛著彼此。Daniel 是我見過最善良的人，我衷心相信是他影響了我成為一個更好的人。我不曾懷疑他對我的愛和忠誠⋯⋯可是，今天我發現他出軌了。

我大約在三星期前已開始有所懷疑。我當時在洗澡，在去水口發現了一些絕對不屬於我或 Daniel 的東西。

我大哭起來，並立即跑出去質問他。我甚至在他面前揮舞這該死的東西，他半點都沒有退縮。他完全不屑一顧！他告訴我不要太擔心，然後就離開了房間。

那次之後，我注意到 Daniel 有時會衣衫不整。你要知道，他是一個非常整潔、很有條理的人，所以這樣極不尋常。那刻，我肯定他和其他女人鬼混了。最糟糕的是⋯⋯他身上有那個女人的味道！

每次我質問他，他都會扯開話題，或只是嚴厲地看著我。他一百八十度轉變的態度簡直要把我逼瘋了。

After weeks of crying my heart out, I decided to stop being helpless and take action to confirm my suspicions. I ventured into the basement where I definitely heard the voice of another woman.

And finally, I saw *her*.

She was young and only had one blue eye — the exact same shade as the one that I found in the shower drain. Her face was caked with dirt and dried blood which had flowed from her empty eye socket. She looked at me pleadingly, struggling to speak as her mouth was gagged and her limbs were chained to the wall. Her naked body was a canvas of bruises, nauseating infections and angry red burns.

Dirty bitch.

It was ME who Daniel chose to live with him forever. Years of being by his side (only his alone!), and she dare try to take my place?

I couldn't help it. Anger blinded me as I wrapped my hands around her neck. I squeezed as hard as I could, watching her squeal and wriggle like the pig she was until she stopped breathing.

我哭得肝腸寸斷，哭了幾星期之後，就決定不再坐以待斃，要採取實際行動證明我的猜測。我小心翼翼地走進地下室，我確切聽見了另一個女人的聲音從這裡傳出來。

終於，我見到了她。

她很年輕，只有一隻藍眼睛——和我在去水口發現的那隻一樣顏色。她的臉沾滿了污垢，還有從她空洞的眼窩裡流出來、已乾涸的血跡。嘴巴被塞住無法作聲、四肢被鎖在牆上的她用懇求的眼神看著我。她赤裸的身體滿佈瘀傷、噁心的傷口感染，還有鮮紅燒傷。

骯髒的婊子。

Daniel 選擇了**我**永遠和他一起生活。我陪伴在他身邊多年（只有我一個人！），她現在膽敢想搶我的位置？

我忍無可忍。我被憤怒蒙蔽了雙眼，用雙手圍住她的脖子，用盡全力擠壓，看著她像頭豬一樣尖叫和扭動，直到她停止呼吸。

Though... there's one thing I realised. When he first brought me home years ago, he didn't throw the eye he plucked from me down the drain. I guess that means he loves me, or at least, more than he loves her!

I don't think I can live without him...

我還意識到一件事。幾年前他第一次帶我回家時，雖然他挖掉我的眼睛，但沒有把它扔到去水口。我想這意味著他很愛我，或者至少他愛我多過愛她！

我覺得沒有他我就活不下去了……

Man Up

I wiped my tears as the truck rumbled to a stop in the empty field.

"Dad?" I hiccupped. "Aren't we going to the vet?"

"I didn't say we were going to the vet." He shook his head. "I said we're gonna put the damned dog down."

I patted the yellow Labrador in my lap. Maggie was older than me; She'd been beside me my whole life. She was a good dog, but she was in pain. Her achy joints prevented her from being a hunting dog anymore, and she was too slow to catch any vermin around the crops. She stopped being a good worker, but she had never stopped being my best friend.

Another wave of tears washed over me as I tried to help her out of the truck.

"Quit your crying." Dad said as he picked the dog up and started walking through the field. I followed him, already sweating as the hot July sun beat down on me.

"You cry at every damn thing. Need to toughen up a bit." He put her down and told her to sit, and walked away to put a few feet's worth of distance between us. He pulled a pistol out of his pocket.

拿出男子氣概

貨車隆隆地停在空曠的田野，我擦乾了眼淚。

「爸爸？」我打著嗝說：「我們不是去看獸醫嗎？」

「我沒說我們要去看獸醫。」他搖搖頭，「我說我們要把那該死的狗解決掉。」

我拍了拍趴在我腿上的金毛拉布拉多犬 Maggie。牠比我年長，而且一直都在我身邊。Maggie 是隻很乖的狗狗，但牠很痛苦。牠的關節痛使牠無法再當獵犬，而且牠的速度太慢了，連農田的害蟲都再也捕捉不到。Maggie 雖然不再是個好幫手，但牠一直都是我最好的朋友。

我想扶牠下貨車時，淚水再次湧出來。

「別哭了。」爸爸邊說邊抱起狗狗，邁步走到田野裡。七月的烈日把跟在爸爸身後的我照得大汗淋漓。

「你無論甚麼屁事都要哭，要堅強一點才行。」爸爸放下 Maggie，叫牠坐下，然後走遠，讓我們和牠之間保持幾英尺的距離。接著他從口袋裡掏出一把手槍。

"You're going to shoot her?" I asked, panicked.

"Nope." He said, handing me the gun. "You're going to shoot her."

I stared at him, mouth agape, waiting for him to tell me that this was a poor-taste joke and to get back in the truck.

"We do this with all the dogs. A bullet is cheaper than a trip to the vet, and she won't feel a thing."

"I don't want to."

"Well that's too damn bad. This is the perfect opportunity to expose you to some real-world problems. Coddled kids become soft adults. I did it as a boy too, helps you man up."

I stared at the pistol in my hand. I had seen animals that were shot while dad hunts. It's a flashy and gorey death. It's not a death she deserved. I couldn't believe he would let this happen to her, that he would make this happen to her.

"Well, go on," he nodded his head towards the dog, "You need to know how to get through tough sh*t. We can get an ice cream when you're done."

「你要向牠開槍？」我驚慌失措地問。

「不是。」他邊說邊把槍遞給我，「是你要向牠開槍。」

我目瞪口呆地望著他，等著他告訴我這是一個低俗的笑話，然後回到貨車上。

「我們對所有狗都是這樣做的。一顆子彈比去看獸醫還便宜，而且牠不會有任何感覺。」

「我不想。」

「呃，那真是太糟糕了。這是個讓你接觸現實世界難題的大好機會。嬌生慣養的孩子會變成軟弱的大人。我小時候也這樣做過，這能激發你的男子氣概。」

我盯著手中的手槍。我有見過爸爸打獵時射殺的動物，牠們死得痛快但很血腥。Maggie 不應該這樣死去。我不敢相信爸爸竟然會讓這件事發生在 Maggie 身上，不敢相信他竟然就是促成這件事的人。

「喂，來吧，」他朝狗狗點了點頭，「你要學會如何渡過難關。你辦好之後我們可以去買雪糕吃。」

Maybe it was the blaring sun or the sweat in my eyes, but I didn't recognize the man standing in front of me. He looked at me expectantly, impatient for me to slaughter my best friend. I looked back at him, trying to take control of my breath.

I aimed and pulled the trigger.

I lay down next to my dog and hugged her. She licked the meat and blood on my arms. I didn't care that I didn't have a way home, or that the heat was making me dizzy, or that the birds were already circling us above. I only cared that she was still alive, and I couldn't have been happier.

或許是烈日太耀眼，或許是汗水流到眼睛，我對站在我面前的這個人很陌生。他滿懷期待地看著我，迫不及待地想我殺掉我最好的朋友。我回頭看著他，努力控制呼吸。

我瞄準並扣動了扳機。

我躺在狗狗旁邊，抱了抱牠。牠舔了舔我手臂上的血肉。我已經不在乎我要怎樣走回家，或是使我頭昏腦脹的酷熱，又或是在我們上方盤旋的鳥兒。我只在乎 Maggie 還活著，我就再高興不過了。

Twins

Kiersi and I were born identical. From birth, people confused us. We dressed alike, styled our hair the same way, and we even had that twin stereotype 'secret language'.

When puberty hit and we got to high school, we simply fell out of sync. We were still identical, of course. It's just that Kiersi wanted to *try* and I just… didn't. I wasn't depressed, I wasn't even unhappy, it's just that she was SO happy. It showed. It reflected in everything. She knew everyone and was genuinely friends with them. She dressed well, took detailed care of her waist-length hair, had a skincare routine that kept her looking like a freshly picked peach. She had a boyfriend! We had the same face, I had no trouble getting boys to look at me, but they didn't look at me the way Adam looked at her.

In saying all this, I can recognize how jealous I may sound, but rest assured that simply isn't the case. I looked up to Kiersi as we grew up. I cut my hair short and dressed casually for ease because I was lazy, but I admired her ability to do it all and make it look so effortless. I wasn't even jealous of her relationship. I was happy to know someone looked at her like I did, like the sun shone from her very pores.

Admiration simply wasn't enough. I wanted to do more for myself, instead of just watching it happen.

形影不離

我和 Kiersi 是對雙胞胎。從小到大，其他人都分辨不到我們兩人。我們衣著相似，留著相同的髮型，我們之間甚至有那種雙胞胎刻板印象的「秘密語言」。

上了高中、踏入青春期的我們不再同步了。當然我們仍然長得一模一樣，只是 Kiersi 想作出新嘗試，但我不想。我沒有因此感到沮喪，我甚至沒有不開心，只是她太開心了。太明顯了，一切都反映著我們的差別。她跟每個人都很要好，而且和他們是真正交心的朋友。Kiersi 穿著得體，留著一把精心打理的及腰長髮，護膚程序更是一絲不苟，臉蛋白裡透紅得像剛摘下的桃子。她交男朋友了！我們長著同一張臉，男孩們也會看我，但他們看我的眼神跟 Adam 看 Kiersi 的眼神不一樣。

在說以上這些話時，我知道聽起來我很妒忌她，但請放心，事實並非如此。在我們長大的過程中，我視 Kiersi 為榜樣。因為懶惰，我剪了短髮，穿著亦很隨意。但我很佩服她那麼用心，而且看起來毫不費力。我也沒有妒忌她有交往對象。我很高興知道有人會用跟我一樣的愛慕眼神看 Kiersi，她整個人就像陽光從毛孔裡照出來一樣閃閃發亮。

只是欽佩她並不足夠。我想為自己做更多，而不是眼巴巴看著事情一件件發生。

Kiersi was so happy when I asked for her help. She, too, wanted us to be true twins again. To confuse people who didn't know us, to be each other's mirror. She took me to the store immediately and we got started. I learned her skincare routine and we did it together every night, laughing about the day's events over the double bathroom sink. I let my hair grow out, and she got hers cut a bit shorter. In almost no time, we were back where we were as kids, identical in every way, walking arm in arm.

The accident was devastating. Brake failure. Her car wrapped around a tree. You don't truly understand mortality until you see your own face in a casket. The funeral home did the best they could, but you could tell where they had to reconstruct our face, where it had smashed into the steering wheel, where the tree had bashed our skull in.

What was harder was seeing my name on the tombstone, in the obituaries. My accomplishments listed and celebrated as something of the past. I almost regretted switching our licenses, asking her to take my car for the night.

But as I look up into Adam's eyes, bury myself in his warm chest, as he tells me how sorry he is...

It's completely worth it.

當我向 Kiersi 提出這個請求時，她非常高興。她也希望我倆能再次成為真正的雙胞胎——混淆那些不熟悉我們的人，成為彼此的鏡子。她馬上帶我去逛街，開始了我們的改造大計。我跟她學了護膚程序，我們每晚都一起護膚，在浴室的雙鋅盤前大笑著談論當天發生的事情。我把頭髮留長，她把頭髮剪短。我們很快又回到了小時候的模樣，各方面都完全相同，手挽著手走路。

一場意外就毀了一切。刹車掣失靈，她的車子撞得繞著樹幹。直到在棺材裡看見自己的臉，你才真正體會死亡是怎麼一回事。殯儀館的人員盡了最大努力重建 Kiersi 的臉，但你仍可以看出哪裡撞上了軚盤，以及頭骨猛撼樹幹的痕跡。

更讓我痛心的是在墓碑上、訃告上看見自己的名字。我的成就被歌頌，然後被列為過去，成為歷史。我差點就為我們交換駕照，並要求她開我的車過夜的事而感到後悔。

但當我抬頭看著 Adam 的雙眼，將臉埋在他溫暖的胸膛裡，然後他告訴我他有多麼難過的時候⋯⋯

這一切都太值得了。

Portion Control

"Are you sure you want to eat all that?"

The question was posed gently, but still felt like a punch to my gut. My husband stood behind me and rubbed my shoulders supportively as I slowly downsized the portions on my plate. He was right, of course. I was being childish. It had been a few months now, and the baby weight was stubbornly hanging on.

Tim was only helping me be the best version of myself. My initial hurt transformed into the usual nagging guilt, I did spend a lot of time gazing at my little daughter. I knew I could use that time to work out and better myself, but I couldn't help being amazed by her little details. The plump tiny toes, the small bump of a nose, her squishy little thighs.

We named her Clara, but I called her Clary. Tim wanted to help me get back on track. Of course, I also hadn't failed to notice how his face changed when he looked at my stomach or my stretch marks. He'd never admit it, but disgust lurked in his eyes in those moments, and I felt him pulling away. I sighed and scraped more untouched food back. Tim glowed and pulled me close, whispering "I'm really proud of you."

Hope bloomed in my chest.

份量管制

「你確定要吃這麼多嗎？」

這個問題看似很溫和，但我聽著就像被狠狠打了一拳。我慢慢縮小碟子裡的食物份量，丈夫就站在我身後，揉著我的肩膀表示支持。理所當然地，他是對的，而我很幼稚。現在已經過了幾個月，產後的我體重還是頑固地沒有減輕。

Tim 只是幫助我變成最好的自己。最初我覺得很受傷，後來漸漸變成了揮之不去的內疚感，因為我的確花了很多時間注視著小女兒。我知道那段時間明明可以用來鍛鍊身體，讓自己變得更好，但我不禁一直欣賞她身上的小細節——豐滿的小腳趾、隆起的小鼻子、柔軟的小大腿。

我們給她取名叫 Clara，但我叫她 Clary。Tim 想幫助我重回正軌。當他看著我的肚子或妊娠紋時，我當然也注意到他臉色的變化。雖然他從不承認，但從那些時刻他眼神中潛藏著的厭惡，我感覺到他漸行漸遠。我嘆了口氣，把更多沒吃過的食物盛回去。Tim 喜形於色，把我拉近並低聲說：「我為你感到很驕傲。」

我心中燃起了一線希望。

Within weeks, my friends and family noticed a difference, my friends gushed about how easily I lost the baby weight. Tim came back to me, I felt sexy and proud. Before long, I reached my goal weight, but Tim encouraged me to keep going. Another five pounds. Then another. It seemed the less of me there was, the more of me he wanted. My friends stopped gushing and started giving me worried looks instead, so I stopped seeing them. It was okay, I had Tim, and my little Clary.

It was almost time for my weekly weigh-in with Tim, but I had to get lunch ready for Clary first. Tim had suggested it as a way to up my awareness of my body. It was humiliating, but I could see his point. When he showed me all the extra inches it had been really motivating to try even harder.

Tim came into the kitchen as I was getting the food onto Clary's plate. She was growing into such a sweet, healthy girl, and I still loved to squeeze her squishy little thighs.

Tim stopped and stared disapprovingly at her plate.

"Do you really think she should eat all that?"

After he left I stared at Clary for a long time, then at my reflection in the kitchen window.

幾週之內，朋友和家人就注意到我瘦了。朋友們滔滔不絕地談論我輕輕鬆鬆就修身成功。Tim 回到了我身邊，重拾性感的我感到自豪。不久後，我達到了目標體重，但 Tim 鼓勵我繼續堅持下去，再減五磅，達成之後又再多減五磅。彷彿我的體重越輕，他就越覺得我重要。朋友們不再談論我，而是開始用擔心的眼神看著我，所以我不再與他們見面了。沒關係，我還有 Tim 和小 Clary。

快到我和 Tim 每週的磅重時間了，但我要先為 Clary 準備午餐。Tim 建議我每週磅重來作為提高我對自己身體認識的一種方式。這令我很難堪，但我明白他的用意。他向我展示我減去了多少吋時，這真的很能激勵我更加努力減重。

當我把食物盛到 Clary 的盤子時，Tim 走進了廚房。她正在成長，做一個甜美又健康的女孩，我還是很喜歡捏捏她柔軟的小大腿。

Tim 停了下來，不滿地盯著 Clary 的碟子。

「你真的認為她應該吃那麼多嗎？」

他離開後，我盯著 Clary 看了很久，然後又望向了廚房窗戶裡自己的倒影。

The police looked for a long time, but eventually the missing person's case went cold. People felt sorry for me, but I was okay, I had what I needed.

Clary giggled next to me as we enjoyed our second slice of pizza. Turns out after all, the only thing I needed to lose was Tim.

警方努力找了好一段時間，最終這個列作失蹤人士的案件還是不了了之。人們為我感到難過，但我沒事，我已經有我需要的東西了。

我們一起吃著第二片薄餅，Clary 在我旁邊咯咯地笑著。畢竟，我唯一需要減掉的，就是 Tim。

Sometimes I Just Know Things

Sometimes they're practical things, like *don't take the I-94, there's bad traffic.*

Sometimes they're personal things, like *grandma hid our presents in the shed.*

But then there's something else. Something different.

On TV, psychic visions are such an ordeal — full-body episodes that any sane person would mistake for a seizure.

In fact, it's just a subtle shift.

When we play hide-and-seek, for example — I don't have a full-blown vision of Marianne hiding in the tunnel slide.

Nor does a voice whisper in my ear, "Marianne is in the tunnel slide"

No. Time slows down, every hair on my body stands on end. The word is in my mind the way the answer to a question would be — *tunnel slide.*

靈敏第六感

有時是實際資訊，比如*不要走 I-94 公路，那邊堵車很嚴重*。

有時會是私事，比如*嬤嬤把我們的禮物藏了在棚屋裡*。

但還有其他東西。一些不同的資訊。

電視節目都把通靈現象表現成是一種折磨——全身顫抖，使得任何理智的人都會誤認為是癲癇發作。

事實上，只是抽離一陣子。

例如，我們玩捉迷藏時，我腦袋裡不會有 Marianne 躲在隧道滑梯裡的畫面。

也沒有聲音在我耳邊低語說「Marianne 在隧道滑梯裡」。

這些都沒有。只是時間變慢了，我身上的每一根汗毛都豎了起來。然後我腦海就會回應我的問題，浮現答案——*隧道滑梯*。

I was twelve years old when it happened. Time slowed so much that I felt I was being dragged through it. Ringing filled both of my ears, and my face burned. The guiding force that had led me through childhood was giving me a word I had never heard before: "*Predator.*"

Turning away from my book, I looked up and saw the man staring at me. Staring in the way grown adult men shouldn't stare at 12-year-old girls.

I left the park and found a busy street to walk down on my way home.

Who knows why the word "*karaoke*" floated through my head on a Thursday evening during midterms? Wouldn't it be irresponsible to abandon studying for a random activity I have no interest in?

Well, I met my husband that night.

The guiding force changed for a little while there — through the first eleven years of my daughter's life, it was never anything more than *buy her that toy* or *Gabby will want Mac and Cheese.*

事情發生的時候我才十二歲。時間變得緩慢，慢得令我覺得自己被拖著走。耳朵嗡嗡作響，臉頰熱得滾燙。這個帶領我渡過童年的第六感，當時給了我一個我從未聽過的詞匯——*不懷好意的人*。

我把視線從書上移開，抬頭看到那個男人正盯著我看。一個成年男子不應該用這樣的眼神望著一個十二歲的女孩。

我離開公園，找了一條繁忙的街道走回家。

期中考試的一個星期四晚上，為甚麼「卡拉 OK」這個詞匯會在我腦海中浮現？為了一個我不感興趣的即興活動而放棄學習，不是很不負責任嗎？

這個嘛，我就是在那天晚上認識了現在的丈夫。

有一段時間，第六感發生了一點變化——在照顧女兒的這十一年裡，除了*給她買玩具*，或者 *Gabby 會想吃芝士通心粉*之外甚麼都沒有。

Then, one day, as I was picking Gabby up from school (*go get her early*), that feeling I hadn't felt in twenty years snuck up and sucker-punched me. I heard a roaring in my ears and my vision shifted to red. Time ground to a standstill. It was screaming that word again. The one that makes my stomach turn, ever since that day in the park.

PREDATOR. PREDATOR. P R E D A T O R.

It pulled my vision violently, away from the receptionist and towards the door, where I could see him staring at Gabby.

My blood turned to liquid nitrogen.

Martin Andersen. The school janitor.

Sometimes I just know things.

Sometimes they're personal things, like *Martin drives a green Jeep*.

Sometimes they're practical things, like *clip this one to cut the brake line*.

But then there's that something else.

Something different.

直到有一天，我去學校接 Gabby（*早點去接她*），二十年來沒有再出現的那種感覺悄悄襲來，狠狠轟炸著我腦袋。耳邊傳來一陣轟鳴，我眼前的景象變成了紅色，時間停滯不前，腦袋又閃現著那個詞匯。從那天在公園開始，那個讓我反胃的人。

不懷好意的人。不懷好意的人！不懷好意的人！！！

這次我抽離得很猛烈，彷彿有股力量使我別過頭，不再望著學校的接待員，而是轉向門口，我看到他正盯著 Gabby。

我全身血液彷彿瞬間凝結了。

Martin Andersen。學校那個清潔工。

有時我的第六感就是會提供一些資訊。

有時會是私事，比如 *Martin* 的車是輛綠色吉普車。

有時會是實用的資訊，比如剪掉這個來切斷剎車系統。

但還有其他東西。

一些不同的資訊。

AITA for
Not Letting My Daughter Cry?

From a very young age, I've ingrained this rule into Irene's head that no matter what happens, however upset she gets over anything or anyone, she can never cry about it.

Nobody overcomes their problems by getting all teary-eyed and depressed about it. It makes you weak. You've just got to accept a bad situation, smile, and get on with your life… right?

And yes, it is impossible to ensure that someone *never* gets upset. But I've done everything in my capacity to stop Irene from crying. I buy her all the toys and trinkets she wants. When I sense something's troubling her, I tell her a joke, sing a song, or come up with some other antic to distract her from what's distressing her.

Things went south (literally) when we had to move places due to my work. Irene couldn't be home-schooled anymore, so I enrolled her in the fanciest private school. But the kids in her grade were anything but fancy. They wouldn't stop giggling about her 'weird' accent or how her hair looked 'odd'.

It got to Irene; she would run back home, pouting and complaining about the jokes made at her expense. Offering gifts didn't seem to make her happy anymore. I was running out of *my* jokes to tell her.

不讓女兒哭的壞媽媽

從 Irene 還很小的時候，我就開始在她腦袋裡植根了這條規則：無論發生甚麼事，無論遇到令她有多難過的人和事，她都不可以哭。

淚流滿面和鬱鬱寡歡不能助你克服難題，只會讓你變得懦弱。而你只需要接受現實有多糟糕，面帶微笑地繼續生活下去，對吧？

的而且確，人不可能永遠都不會難過，但我已盡我所能阻止 Irene 哭泣。她想要甚麼玩具、小飾物，我都買給她。要是我感覺到她有事煩心，我就會給她講個笑話、唱首歌，或者想出一些滑稽動作來分散她的注意力，讓她不再想著困擾她的事情。

為了工作，我們搬到南邊，一切卻變得糟糕。Irene 不能再在家上學了，所以我讓她就讀了區內最好的私立學校。但她的同學卻一點也不好，只顧不停笑她的口音「怪異」，又說她的髮型很「奇怪」。

這讓 Irene 傷心透了；她會跑回家，噘著嘴抱怨別人拿她開玩笑。送禮物給她似乎不再能讓她開心了，我也快沒有笑話可以逗她笑了。

I decided that getting Irene to talk to a shrink about her troubles could make her happier.

The shrink believed that Irene was withholding herself too much; she was suppressing her emotions, which wasn't healthy. So, the next time Irene feels upset, she should try dealing with the sadness instead.

I knew nothing of this closed-door conversation between Irene and her shrink. Not until Irene returned home from school one day- crying her eyes out because the cheerleader who had called her ugly that day had fallen off the pyramid and broken a leg.

Some days later, the resident school bully who had also made my Irene cry- broke his wrist, punching a locker.

Things came to a head during her recital. Irene forgot her lines and got some smirks from the crowd. When I found her crying in the green room, a fire had broken out in the theatre. No one got hurt, thankfully, but this was too close.

On our way back, I gave Irene a real hard time for crying. I had always taught her to be strong, be happy. But she chose to dwell on her sadness, which made her weak and caused her to cry. I let my disappointment be known.

我決定讓 Irene 和心理醫生訴說一下她的煩惱，希望可以讓她更快樂。

心理醫生認為 Irene 太克制自己了，她在壓抑自己的情緒，這樣不健康。所以下次 Irene 感到難過時，她應該試著去處理悲傷的情緒。

我本來並不知道 Irene 和心理醫生之間那次閉門談話的內容，直到有一天 Irene 放學回家——那天罵她醜的啦啦隊長從疊羅漢頂層上掉下來摔斷了腿，她哭得唏哩哇啦。

幾天後，學校裡那個無人不知的惡霸——他也弄哭了我的 Irene——在用拳頭打向儲物櫃時，折斷了手腕。

在她的朗誦會上，這件事的嚴重性變得不容忽視。Irene 忘詞了，人群中發出了一些竊笑聲。當我發現她在演員休息室裡哭泣時，劇院著火了。幸好沒有人受傷，真的很險。

回家路上，我因為 Irene 最近常常在哭的事，嚴厲地教訓了她。我一直教導她要堅強、要快樂，但她卻選擇沉浸在悲傷中，使她軟弱，也使她哭泣。我表達了我有多失望。

Looking back, I should've patiently explained our family's curse to her, which made her crying so dangerous for others.

My stomach dropped when I heard her ghastly sobs from the backseat. Irene regarded me with pitch-black eyes, blood-red tears streaming down her cheeks. It was too late until I realized my daughter was wailing for what, instead, *whom.*

The last thing I saw in the flare of the approaching truck's headlights was a sinister smile on Irene's crying face.

現在回想起來，我應該耐心地向她解釋我們家的詛咒，她的哭泣會令其他人陷入危險。

我聽見後座傳來Irene淒慘的抽泣聲，我的胃頓時扭成一團。Irene用漆黑的雙眼盯著我看，血紅的淚水順著臉頰流下。我本來在想女兒到底為了甚麼事在哭，但當我意識到她原來是為*誰*而哭時，一切都太遲了。

在駛近的貨車車頭燈的映照下，眼前的最後一個畫面，是Irene哭泣的臉上露出陰險的笑容。

Became Homeless in Five Easy Steps

Step 1.

Lana was late for work that morning so she was driving a little frantically, swerving left and right on the road without signaling and, naturally, she ended up cutting off a few cars along the way, receiving angry beeps from the vehicles.

One of the offended drivers was Mr. Pakovic, a very wealthy man whose success in life was based largely on being ruthless and vindictive. Later that day Pakovic made some inquiries about the rude driver of the car that annoyed him - the type of inquiry that only the rich people can make. The fact that Lana's car had a memorable number plate, "BUSSIN", helped him with his cause.

Among the findings was Lana's place of work and, as it turns out, Pakovic was a large client of the company. A few phone calls later, Lana lost her job.

Step 2.

Having been laid off for a "mysterious" reason Lana went home all dejected, stopping at a gas station on the way. Then, at the cashier came another humiliation of having her card declined. How can this be?

流浪的捷徑

第一步：

Lana 那天早上上班要遲到了，所以她有點忙亂地開車，在路上左穿右插，沒有用轉向燈。於是她在路上超了幾輛車插隊，被憤怒的車主叭叭地響鞍警告。

其中一個心有不忿的車主是 Pakovic 先生，他是個富翁，他冷酷無情，而且報復心強，很大程度上造就了他的成功。那天晚些時候，Pakovic 調查了那個讓他惱火的粗魯司機是誰——只有富人才能作出這樣的調查。Lana 有一個很易記的車牌「BUSSIN」，這一點幫助了 Pakovic 的調查。

調查後得知了 Lana 的工作地點，而且 Pakovic 是該公司的大客戶。幾個電話之後，Lana 的飯碗就丟了。

第二步：

因「神秘」原因被解僱後，Lana 沮喪地回家，途中停了在加油站。然後，在收銀台結賬時她的信用卡無法入賬，令她覺得很丟臉。怎麼會這樣？

After scrounging enough cash to pay for the gas she came home to find her credit card had been maxed, on account of a $8,500 purchase of something called "Crypto Forever #bRoS". What can this mean?

Well, it was her son, who used her card so frequently to memorize the numbers and could use it as he wished. "It's an investment," he said.

Step 3.

The purchase was cancelled, but it looked rather unlikely that a refund would be made, the company ceasing to exist and all, shortly after. Meanwhile, Lana's bills weren't being paid, since they were all linked to her credit card account. Lana was at her wit's end.

Step 4.

A foreclosure notice came from the bank. They were taking her house. Unbeknownst to Lana, if the bank finds out you've been fired, it will start taking a closer look at your situation.

And, if you're having problems paying your bills, for example, and your credit score starts dropping, under the mortgage contract the bank can unilaterally put your house up for sale and kick you out.

東拼西湊後，終於籌集到足夠的現金來支付加油費。回到家她發現信用卡已經刷爆了，原因是購買了一個價值 8,500 美元、名為「加密貨幣萬歲」的東西。那是甚麼？

唔，是她兒子，他常常用她的卡，用到把卡號背了起來，想何時刷、怎麼刷都可。「這是一項投資。」他說。

第三步：
購買取消了，但不太可能收到退款，而且不久之後那間公司就消失了。與此同時，Lana 的所有賬單都無法繳費，因為全部都和她的信用卡賬戶連結了。Lana 束手無策。

第四步：
收到來自銀行的喪失抵押品贖回權通知。銀行要收掉 Lana 的房子。她不知道的是，如果銀行發現你被解僱了，他們會開始仔細地審查你。

再者，例如你無法支付賬單，信用評分開始下降時，根據按揭條款，銀行可以單方面出售你的房子，並可以把你趕走。

Banks are like flood water, you feel getting wet and the next thing, you're drowning. Lana had 1 month to come up with the solution.

Step 5.

Lana went to the lawyer. $8,000 retainer if they're going to accept the job. Lana basically went through every character that ever appeared in her life to borrow.

The case proceeded and Lana, very foolishly, fought the bank. It went for six months. The lawyers charged $29,000 by then. She couldn't pay. They dropped the case. The house was sold. With all the fees and charges, the bank's expenses etc. she got $1,200 in her pocket.

At the end, Lana found herself sitting on the curb outside her former house. HOA security came by and moved her on.

銀行就像洪水，在你感覺到被水沾濕的下一瞬間就會被淹死。Lana 有一個月時間想出解決方案。

第五步：
Lana 去找律師。如果律師接下這場官司，Lana 需要付 8,000 美元的聘用金。Lana 基本上向她生命中出現過的每一個人物都借了錢。

官司繼續進行，Lana 與銀行交鋒是非常愚蠢的。官司整整持續了六個月。截至那時，律師向 Lana 收取 29,000 美元的律師費。她付不起，所以律師撤銷了這場官司。房子被銀行賣了，加上所有的費用和銀行的開支等，她還剩下 1,200 美元。

最後，Lana 坐在不再屬於她的房子的路邊。業主立案法團叫保安過來請她離開。

Inescapable Nightmares
難逃夢魘

"You're Not My Wife."

I try to brush it off. "How did you sleep, honey?"

"Shut up. Shut the hell up." He throws his phone at the wall, just above my head; I stiffen.

"You don't even SOUND like her. You don't move like her. I know a f**king demon when I see one."

When he first decided to go back to seminary school, I supported him. He'd never been all that religious until he gave up alcohol; I was just so happy that he'd quit drinking.

His evangelizing caused a bigger and bigger rift between us and our friends and family. I started to feel trapped with him and constantly judged by him, reminded over and over again what my roles as a wife were "according to the word of the Lord, our God".

We had no kids together, I had family a few hours away I could stay with; it just made sense for me to leave.

So, about two years into his Evangelical Theology Program, I informed him that I wanted to separate. He took it surprisingly well; I thought this would be a smooth, amicable divorce.

Then the seizures started.

「你不是我妻子。」

我試著轉換話題:「你睡得好嗎,親愛的?」

「住口。給我閉嘴。」他把手機扔到牆上,差點砸到我的頭──我僵住了。

「你的聲音不像她,舉止也不像她。我一眼就能認出你是個惡魔。」

他當初決定回神學院時,我很支持他。在他戒酒之前,他從來沒有那麼虔誠過。我很高興他戒酒了。

他傳福音,卻導致我們與朋友和家人之間的裂痕越來越大。我開始覺得被他困住了,而且不斷地被他評判,更反覆地提醒我作為妻子的角色是「根據耶和華我們上帝的話」。

我們膝下無兒,我在幾個小時以外的地方有家人,我可以和他們待在一起;我要離開應該不會有甚麼大問題。

所以,他讀了福音神學課程大約兩年後,我告訴他我想分開。他竟欣然接受了,所以我以為離婚過程會很順利,可以和平收場。

然後癲癇發作了。

I'd had them on and off since around when I got married; my GP, half a dozen nurses and a neurologist were all baffled as to where they came from. Eventually it was chalked up to "stress, probably" and I was prescribed anticonvulsants and sedatives.

But Michael hadn't let me leave the house to get my medication. He had long since stopped taking his own — "Christ heals all ills, and to trust the invention of man over the creator himself is sinful". In fact, Michael hadn't allowed me to leave the house at all for weeks.

He left the house claiming to seek a doctor for a home visit and came back with an exorcist. For six days I was tied to a bed and denied food to starve out the demon. I had a burning piece of firewood held to my face to scare the demon out. I was bound and helpless as they poured foul-tasting tinctures into my pried-open mouth, brewed with holy water and herbs thought to be demon-repelling.

After those six days the exorcist left. I looked at him with pleading eyes, begging him without speaking to go to the police. After a few words with Michael, the man left and I was again at the mercy of my overzealous husband.

自從我們結婚後，我就時不時會癲癇發作。我的家庭醫生、六名護士和一名神經科醫生都查不到病因。最終他們只好把它歸結為「可能是壓力」，給我開了抗癲癇藥和鎮靜劑。

但是 Michael 不讓我踏出家門去取藥。他也早就不再吃自己的藥了——「基督治癒所有疾病，相信人類的發明而不是造物主本身是有罪的。」事實上，Michael 已經好幾個星期不讓我出門了。

他說要外出找醫生上門看診，回家時卻帶著驅魔人進來。我整整六天被綁在床上，他們要我絕食來餓死惡魔，又用一塊燒著的木柴抵住我的臉來嚇跑惡魔。他們將難聞的酊劑強行倒進我的嘴裡，被束縛的我很無助，這些酊劑是用聖水和他們認為可以驅魔的草藥釀製的。

那六天之後，驅魔人離開了。我用懇求的眼神看著他，不發一語地求他報警。跟 Michael 聊了幾句，那個人就離開了，我又再次被過分熱心的丈夫擺佈了。

And now said husband is staring at me with the eyes of a lunatic. Wild, primal, and bloodthirsty, as though he were facing the Devil itself.

"Michael, please baby, please believe me," I'm so desperate at this point that I don't consider the hundreds of times I've begged before, or how it just made him angrier.

"Michael, I am your wife. I'm Bridget. I married you in my fathers backyard on 15th March 1995. I design clothing. I love my husband Michael dearly and I. Am. His. Wife. Bridget. Please baby, just let me go" I choke, not realizing I had started to cry.

He opens a large glass bottle and walks over to me. I brace myself for another noxious tincture, but he upends the bottle and pours the strong-smelling clear liquid all over my body.

Alcohol.

"It is by the spirit of God that I cast out the demons," he recites as he pulls out a matchbook. I open my mouth to scream, and he shoves a rag in my mouth, silencing me. "… then the kingdom of God shall come upon you." He lights a match.

Our eyes meet.

現在丈夫正用瘋子的眼光盯著我。狂野、原始、嗜血，彷彿他正面對的是惡魔本身。

「Michael，求求你，寶貝，請相信我，」我絕望得即使知道自己已經乞求過他無數次，知道這會令他更憤怒，我仍要說出口。

「Michael，我是你的妻子，我是 Bridget。1995 年 3 月 15 日，我們在我父親的後院成婚。我設計服裝。我深愛著我丈夫 Michael。我，是，你，妻，子，Bridget。求求你，寶貝，放過我吧。」我哽咽著說，沒有意識到自己在哭。

他打開一個大玻璃瓶，朝我走來。我做好心理準備要喝下另一種有毒的酊劑，但他把瓶子倒轉，把氣味濃烈的透明液體淋在我身上。

酒精。

「我憑借上帝聖靈驅魔，」他拿出火柴盒時背誦道。我張開嘴想尖叫，他就把一塊破布塞進我嘴裡，讓我無法發出聲音。「……神的國度必臨於你。」他點燃了一根火柴。

我們四目交投。

In that look, I can see the truth. Nobody else will, and nobody else would have had I tried to explain. By all outside accounts, my husband is a madman who murdered his wife by accident, believing her to be a demon.

But in that last look, the last time I met my husband's eyes, mine asked a question. As I looked into the crazed, enraged eyes of my killer, I silently asked, "it's all been you, hasn't it? These seizures? This 'demon'? All because I want to leave?"

With the slightest of nods, he drops the match.

This story is inspired by, in memory of, and dedicated to Bridget Cleary (née: Boland), who was murdered by her husband Micheal Cleary on 15th March 1895, allegedly because he believed she had been replaced by a changeling. Bridget was 26 years old when she died.

我從他那眼神中，看到了真相。除了我之外，沒有其他人會知道真相，即使我有機會解釋，也沒有人會相信。在外界看來，丈夫只是個認為妻子是惡魔而誤殺了她的瘋子。

但在最後一次和丈夫對望時，我問了一個問題。當我看著眼前這雙瘋狂又憤怒的眼睛時，我低聲問道：「都是你弄出來的，對嗎？我的癲癇、甚麼『惡魔』？全都只是因為我想離婚？」

他輕輕點了點頭，就把火柴拋下了。

這個故事靈感來自 Bridget Cleary（娘家姓：Boland），並以此紀念她。她於 1895 年 3 月 15 日被丈夫 Micheal Cleary 殺害，據稱是因為 Michael 認為 Bridget 已被換生靈取代。Bridget 去世時年僅二十六歲。

I am a Prisoner

I am a prisoner. My captor seems to delight in my suffering. It is so much larger than I am and it easily picks me up and moves me around. I cannot stand it.

I cannot understand a word it says. Each time I try to plead with my captor for mercy, for kindness my pleas fall on deaf ears. Instead it shouts my words back at me, but wrong. Garbled and twisted, nothing but a mockery of my language.

The meals are equally cruel. Even garbage would be better. My captor acts as if I should be thankful for this swill. But each time I consume it I feel weaker. Perhaps that is its intention.

The weeks continue to bleed past and nothing changes. My captor torments me daily. The treatment I receive is abysmal and the meals are worse. And yet, my captor regales in this. It feels I should be thriving in this horrid place. I cannot fathom it. Yet I only feel my strength fading. To even rise up from the floor I'm kept on is growing difficult.

Once there was a beacon of hope. Another of my captors' kind arrived in the prison where I am kept. It saw me and began yelling at my captor. My captor only screamed back, throwing items from its nest at the newcomer. I still can't understand their tongue, but I can feel the rage my captor was willing to unleash.

囚徒

我淪為了囚徒,而俘虜者似乎以我的痛苦為樂。它體型比我大得多,可以輕易把我抱來抱去。我快要受不了。

它說的話我一個字也聽不懂。每次我試圖向俘虜者求情時,我的請求都被置若罔聞。相反,它會大聲模仿我說話,但它說得亂七八糟、錯漏百出,似是在嘲弄我的語言。

膳食同樣殘酷,垃圾都比我的餐點豐盛。俘虜者表現得我應該感恩可以吃這些像豬食的剩飯菜。但我每次吃完都會感到越來越虛弱。也許它就是想我變成這樣吧。

幾週過去了,仍然一切如舊。俘虜者仍然每天折磨我,我受到的待遇很可怕,飯菜也越來越難吃。然而,俘虜者卻樂此不疲,認為我會在這個可怕的環境下茁壯成長。我無法理解,只覺得自己越來越乏力,站起來都變得越來越困難。

曾經出現過一線曙光——一個俘虜者的同類來到了它關押我的監獄。它看到我之後就對俘虜者大喊大叫。俘虜者只是尖叫回擊,然後從巢穴裡拿東西丟向這個新來的傢伙。

雖然我還是聽不懂它們的語言,但我感覺到俘虜者在發洩它的怒火。

I suppose I will never be free.

This seems to be its wish as I continue to grow weaker by the day. It has been months that I've been in this hell and I do not know how much longer I will last. With each day I grow weaker. Even breathing is becoming difficult.

Perhaps this has made even my captor feel remorse. On a day so much worse than any other I could not even open my eyes. I prayed silently that perhaps this would be the end of this curse. Then I see my captor approach me. Or I think I do. My sight has faded with my strength and will.

My captor places me in an even smaller cell and moves me as if I am nothing. But, for the first time in ages I taste the air as it truly should be. I know that if I had the strength I could escape at this moment, but I also know that I am too far gone.

After what feels like an eternity I am removed from my cell into a strange room. Another of my captors' kind is speaking with it. There is such anger. My captor shrieks. I have never heard such a sound. It grabs me and runs, not even bothering to put me in the cell. Not that I have the energy to escape.

我應該永遠都不會重獲自由了吧。

這似乎是它的心願，因為我仍然日漸虛弱。我在這個地獄已經待了好幾個月，我不知道自己還能堅持多久。日復一日，我每天都變得更虛弱，連呼吸都變得困難。

或許這讓俘虜者感到懊悔了。有一天我史無前例地痛苦，虛弱得連眼睛也無力睜開。我默默祈禱著，心想也許這就是詛咒的終結。然後我看到俘虜者走近了我，又或者是我走近了它吧。我的視力隨著體力和意志一起消退了。

俘虜者把我關在一個更小的牢房裡，好像當我不在裡面般，把我搬來搬去。但是，這是長久以來我第一次真正聞到空氣的味道。我知道如果我還有一絲力氣，我可以在這一刻逃脫，但我也知道，那只是妄想。

感覺像過了一個世紀之後，我從牢房被移到一個陌生的房間。另一個俘虜者的同類正在和它說話，房間裡充斥著憤怒。俘虜者失聲尖叫，那是我從來沒有聽到過的聲音。它抱起我，甚至沒有把我關回牢房，拔腿就跑，雖然我也沒有力氣逃走。

I am brought back to my prison and my captor holds me in the air. It's garbled words I can't understand ringing in my ears. I only wish for quiet. For an end to this suffering.

"That stupid vet doesn't have a clue what he's talking about Mr. Mittens. Of course you can be vegan! Just like Mommy! And I could never give you meat anyway. I can't stand to see an animal suffer."

我被帶回監獄，俘虜者將我舉在空中。耳邊迴盪著我聽不懂的亂碼。我只求安靜，只求結束這場痛苦的折磨。

「那個笨蛋獸醫根本在胡說八道。咪咪先生，你當然可以只吃純素！就像媽媽一樣！而且我永遠也不會給你吃肉，我不忍心看見動物受苦。」

BOOK OF NOTES

Meeting Death Herself is Bad. Near-Death, However, is Much Worse.

Meeting Death Herself is Bad.
Near-Death, However, is Much Worse.

"Holy f**k. That... that was..."

Steven had to pause, had to calm down his racing heart, had to steady his breathing before he fainted from the shock.

It's not every day that your car flips and rolls six times down a hill.

Steven could feel his shirt grow damp; he was bleeding. His arm was also pinned, and his legs were stuck between chunks of crushed metal.

"This... this was your fault. You... hurt... me. Why do you keep hurting me?" Steven called, half-hysteric, into the air. Steven saw feet outside the cab, and for a half-second, almost thought it was someone who'd come to help before he realized who his visitor actually was.

"You're lucky that it's me who does this to you." Near-Death said. "You could be having it so, so much worse right now." Steven didn't respond, and Near-Death was gone by the time Steven heard sirens.

Steven didn't see him again until he was at the hospital.

遇見死神很糟，
但遇見瀕死之神更糟

「他媽的。那、那是……」

Steven 不得不停下來，好讓狂跳的心平復下來，穩定呼吸，好讓自己不會因震驚而暈倒。

車子衝下山坡，翻滾了整整六圈。這些事不會每日都發生。

Steven 感覺到襯衫變得濕答答──他在流血。他的手臂也被釘住，雙腿被壓在金屬碎塊之間。

「這、這是你的錯……你傷害了我……你為甚麼總是在傷害我？」Steven 幾乎歇斯底里地對著空氣喊道。

Steven 看見的士外面有一雙腿，他一度以為有人來幫忙，半秒後就意識到這個訪客到底是誰。

「你真幸運，因為下手的人是我。」瀕死之神說：「要不然你現在的情況可能會更糟。」

Steven 沒有回應。而當 Steven 聽到警笛聲時，瀕死之神已經離開了。

Steven 到醫院後又和祂重遇。

He opened his eyes after a morphine-induced nap, and, at the foot of his bed, stood Near-Death.

He was a pale, relatively average man in height and looks. He had curly, mid-length dark hair, and wore circular, wire-frame glasses and a black turtleneck with leather elbow patches.

"Does it hurt?" He asked, smiling. "Your lung was punctured. Your arm is broken. Of course it does."

"What if... I just squeezed this a little bit, hmm?" He said again, grabbing Steven's oxygen tube in his cold hand and squeezing tightly until the monitors started beeping.

Then he let go.

"I'll see you soon, Steven," he whispered, and vanished as the nurses rushed in.

That hospital visit was the fifth Near-Death experience Steven had had, and that whispered sentence promised many more.

Again and again, Near-Death targeted him, orchestrating event after event of torture.

嗎啡讓他小睡了片刻，他睜開雙眼，就看見瀕死之神正站在床尾。

祂皮膚蒼白，身高和相貌跟一個普通男子無異，頂著一頭捲曲的中長黑髮，戴著圓形幼框眼鏡，身著手肘有皮革貼片的黑色高領毛衣。

「會痛嗎？」祂笑著問道：「你的肺被刺穿了，手臂也斷了，當然痛囉。」

「如果……我稍微擠壓一下呢，嗯？」祂繼續説，用冰冷的手抓起了 Steven 的氧氣喉管，然後緊緊地捏著，直到監測器開始發出嗶嗶聲。

祂才放手了。

「我們很快會再見面喔，Steven。」祂低聲説，然後在護士衝進來時消失了。

這次留院已是 Steven 第五次瀕死體驗，而那句耳語彷彿預示了還會有更多次。

一次又一次，瀕死之神以他為目標，精心策劃著一場又一場的折磨。

BOOK OF NO 4 FEAR

Meeting Death Herself is Bad. Near-Death, However, is Much Worse.

Always enough to agonize; never enough to kill.

Once, Steven tried hiding within his home to avoid all possible danger.

He was shot by a burglar two nights later.

Near-Death was always watching him.

Steven wanted to die. But Near-Death wouldn't let that happen.

The ropes always broke, the police always found him in time.

He was always brought back.

"Please. Stop. Please. I can't do it anymore," Steven begged Near-Death. "Let me die."

"Can't do that. Sorry. But I'll leave you, if that's truly what you want."

"You didn't think I'd leave without a goodbye, did you?" Near-Death said, sitting in a chair in Steven's hospital room.

It was the same hospital as last time, but a different wing.

總是叫人痛不欲生，可是永遠死不去。

有一次，Steven 躲在家裡，希望避免任何危機。

兩天後他被竊賊開槍射傷。

瀕死之神一直監視著他。

Steven 很想死去，但瀕死之神不會允許。

繩子總是會斷掉，警察總能及時找到他。

他總是會在鬼門關被拉回來。

「請你停手，求求你，我捱不下去了，」Steven 向瀕死之神
乞求：「請讓我死去吧。」

「恕難從命。但如果你衷心希望我離開你，我可以照辦。」

「你難道以為我會不辭而別嗎？」瀕死之神坐在 Steven 病房
的椅子上問道。

和上次車禍是同一間醫院，只是不同的翼樓。

The cancer ward.

"Y'know, brain cancer can be incredibly deadly. And incredibly painful."

"Why?" Steven whispered through chapped lips.

Near-Death simply smiled.

"Who knows if you'll die. I'm not gonna be there for that, as per your request."

"Maybe you'll meet Death herself soon. Lovely woman. I'm sure you'll like her."

At those words, Steven, reduced to nothing but chemo-filled agony, closed his eyes.

When they opened, Near-Death was gone.

癌症病房。

「你知道吧，腦癌可能非常致命，而且非常痛苦。」

「為甚麼？」Steven 張著乾裂的雙唇低聲說。

瀕死之神只是笑了笑。

「沒有人知道你會不會死去，但我會按照你的要求，不會陪你走最後一程。」

「也許你很快就會遇到死神，那個可愛的女人。我相信你會喜歡她的。」

聽完這番話，Steven 閉上了眼睛，只剩下化療的痛苦陪伴著他。

當雙眼再次打開時，瀕死之神已經消失了。

This Plane is Going Down

The initial panic already happened. The masks came down. There was screaming and crying and fighting; turbulence inside as much as out. Now, we're just slowly coasting over the Atlantic.

You could sense that something awful was coming well before anything actually happened. That sensation way down deep in your gut, the way animals sense hurricanes. Then there were murmurs down the aisle. *Lost contact...no radio...*

The pilot had come over the intercom then. Some mechanical jargon about thrust, airspeed, engine failure. I didn't understand it, but it didn't matter. We were slowly falling out of the sky over the ocean with no way to let anyone know. We were going to die, and that was that.

Turbulence. Masks down. Help yourself before assisting others.

Now there was just an eerie calm. No one moved for fear they'd drive us down faster. Or maybe hoped that our stillness would buy us time for someone to find us, to hear us.

The woman across the aisle whispers to her husband about terrorists. He sat facing forward in stone silence. If it hadn't been for his near imperceptible nods, I'd have thought he simply couldn't hear her.

飛機墜毀前

最怕的事發生了。氧氣面罩落下來了。尖叫、哭泣、打鬥；機艙內的動盪跟機艙外的亂流一樣顛簸。我們正在大西洋上空緩慢地航行著。

在一些可怕事情發生之前，你總會感覺得到它即將要發生。這種直覺彷彿與生俱來，就如動物能感知颱風即將來襲。然後通道上傳來竊竊私語。*失去聯繫……無線電沒有訊號……*

接著機師的聲音從對講機傳出。甚麼推力、空速、引擎故障的一堆術語。我聽不懂，但沒關係。我們正慢慢從海洋上空墜落，而且無法與外界聯繫。我們快要死了，就是這樣。

不穩定氣流。氧氣罩落下。先顧好自己，再協助其他人。

現在機艙平靜得詭異。沒人敢動，生怕會加速飛機墜落。或是大家希望靜止不動就能爭取更多時間，好讓有人找到我們，聽見我們的聲音。

通道對面的女人向丈夫低聲談論恐怖分子，丈夫面朝前方，一言不發。要不是他似有還無地點點頭，我還以為他根本沒有聽見她說話。

A baby a few rows up began crying.

I thought about my wife. Didn't that guy in 9/11 leave his wife a voicemail? I checked my phone. *No reception.* I put it away.

The woman next to me shifted her rosary between her fingers.

"Hail Mary, full of grace"

The beads clicked. The sound was impossibly loud in the silence.

"The Lord is with thee"

The baby cried again, shushed by his mother between her own quiet sobs.

"Blessed are thou among women, and blessed is the fruit of thy womb"

Outside the window, the ocean moved closer. A few people buckled their seatbelts. A few unbuckled them.

"Holy Mary, mother of God"

前幾排有個嬰兒哭了起來。

我想起了妻子。911 事件中的那個人在他妻子的語音信箱留了言。我檢查電話,*沒有訊號*,我就把它收起來了。

我旁邊的女人正在用手指撥動手上的念珠。

「*萬福瑪利亞,妳充滿恩寵*」

念珠咔嗒作響,咔嗒聲在寂靜中響亮得誇張。

「*主與妳同在*」

嬰兒又哭了起來,母親壓低自己抽泣聲的同時,試著讓孩子保持安靜。

「*妳在婦女中受讚頌,妳的親子耶穌同受讚頌*」

窗外的大海景色越來越近。有幾個人繫好安全帶,有些人則解開了。

「*天主聖母瑪利亞*」

The woman who had been speaking across the aisle went silent as her husband softly grabed her hand.

"Pray for us sinners"

The beads clicked again and I looked at my phone. No reception.

"Now and in the hour of our death"

The baby's sobs were muffled for a short time, then stopped. The mother sobbed again, louder.

"Amen."

在走道對面的那個丈夫輕輕握住了妻子的手，原本一直在說話的她沉默下來。

「*求妳現在和我們臨終時*」

念珠的咔嗒聲再次響起。我看了看手機。沒有訊號。

「*為我們罪人祈求天主*」

嬰兒的哭聲被抑制住了一小會兒就停止了。然後媽媽又抽泣起來，哭得比之前更大聲了。

「*阿們。*」

Our King is Just. Surely He Must Be.

The whispers of plague started months ago. An illness that sneaks in and drains you of life. It was just rumors at first, then the whispers grew louder.

Even out here in our isolated little village we heard the tales. Once infected, a person had mere hours. There were stories of how fast it spread. That entire village could be wiped out in days.

We took the rumors to heart. Our village was already isolated, so completely closing ranks wasn't difficult. No one was allowed in, the stray merchant or traveler stopped at the gates and made to leave. If you chose to leave, you could not come back. Though some made this choice, refusing to live in fear of a thing they couldn't see.

The months stretched on and our stores grew thin, but still the whispers from the capital came through. Knights would burn entire villages, towns, cities that were thought to be infected.

We worried for those who had left but quietly revelled in our safety. For nearly a year, no one had crossed our borders. Still the plague persisted. So did our village.

瘟疫蔓延

幾個月前開始傳出有關瘟疫的謠言，説那個疾病會無聲入侵身體，然後榨乾你的性命。一開始只是「聽聞」，後來越傳越像真的。

謠言更傳到我們這條非常偏僻的小村子——一旦被感染，就活不過幾個小時；瘟疫傳播速度奇快，幾天就可以殲滅整條村莊。

我們將謠言牢記在心。這條村子本來就與世隔絕，要我們齊心防疫並不困難。沒有人可以進村，迷路的商人或旅行者會被拒諸門外，不能逗留。如果你選擇離開，就不能回來。有些人做出了這個選擇，是因為他們拒絕生活在看不見的恐懼之中。

幾個月過去了，村裡的店舖越來越少，來自首都的謠言仍未間斷——騎士會焚燒認為已被感染的村莊、城鎮、城市。

我們很擔心那些離開了的人，但同時也悄悄地陶醉在安然無恙的環境之中。已將近一年沒有人越過村子的界線，但瘟疫仍然存在，我們的村莊也沒甚改變。

It has now been nearly two full years since the first whispers. We all grew more fearful by the day. We worried if our stores would keep us through another winter. We worried all would be for naught. The slightest illness and we all ran to our homes, precaution turned to prison.

Then the knights arrived.

We saw their banners on the horizon long before they reached the gates. We knew that they were inspecting all the king's lands, to see if the plague still had root. We were proud though. Our precautions were enough and not a single citizen of our town was ill.

The knights set their torches to our homes anyway. The screaming of adults, children, and animals all bled together in my ears. I ran to the closest knight just as he felled another of my neighbors.

"Please, My Lord! I beg of you! No one here is infected, there is no plague here!"

"There never was. There's just too damn many of you insects."

自第一次聽到謠言以來，已經快兩年了。我們每天都變得更加恐懼，擔心自己的店能否支撐我們度過下一個冬天，擔心一切都會化為泡影。即使有那麼一點點不適，我們都會馬上跑回家。防疫措施彷彿將村子變成了監獄般。

然後騎士到來了。

他們還未到達村子大門前，我們就看到了他們的旗幟在地平線冒出。我們知道騎士要檢查所有土地，看看瘟疫是否仍然存在。我們很自豪，因為我們的防疫措施很完善，鎮上沒有一個市民生病。

不過，騎士還是拿起火把燒了我們的家。大人、小孩、動物的慘叫聲轟炸著我的耳朵。當離我最近的騎士擊倒另一名鄰居時，我跑向他。

「求求您，騎士大人！我求您了！這裡沒有人受感染，這裡沒有瘟疫！」

「瘟疫不曾存在。只是你們這些蟲子太多罷了。」

Jeremy

METROPOLITAN POLICE, SOUTHERN DISTRICT.
RECORD OF INTERVIEW.
BEGIN TRANSCRIPT.

DSI JOHNS: This is a recording of an interview with Jeremy Staunton at 6 pm, Tuesday, 12th of June 2021. Present are DSI[1] Miles Johns, along with DS[2] Ken Smiley. Now, Mr. Staunton, we'll begin with your date of birth, address and occupation.

JEREMY: My name is Jeremy Thomas Staunton. I was born on 17th of April 1999. I live with my mum on 13 Calloway Street in Bexley. I am a pizza delivery man.

DSI JOHNS: Ok. Mr. Staunton, could you tell me where you were on the night of 9th of June 2021?

JEREMY: I finished work around 9 pm. Then Tom, my mate at work, and I went to a pub on Wheeler Street.

DSI JOHNS: How long did you stay in the pub?

---

1   DSI : The Department of Special Investigation

2   DS : Detective Sergeant

薄餅速遞員

大都會警察局，南區分部。
會面記錄。
逐字稿開始。

DSI Johns： 現在是 2021 年 6 月 12 日，星期二，下午六點，這是對 Jeremy Staunton 的會面錄音。在場有特別調查科 (DSI) 的 Miles Johns 和偵探警長 Ken Smiley。好的，Staunton 先生，請報上你的出生日期、地址和職業。

Jeremy： 我叫 Jeremy Thomas Staunton，1999 年 4 月 17 日出生，現在和媽媽住在貝克斯利區加羅威街 13 號，工作是薄餅速遞員。

DSI Johns： 好的。Staunton 先生，請問 2021 年 6 月 9 日晚上，你在哪裡？

Jeremy： 我晚上九點左右下班。然後和同事 Tom 去了惠勒街的一間酒吧。

DSI Johns： 你在酒吧待了多久？

JEREMY: An hour or so.

DSI JOHNS: Where did you go after that?

JEREMY: Tom and I went to visit Mrs. Lavalier at
               Caulfield Street.

DSI JOHNS: What was the purpose of the meeting
               with Mrs. Lavalier?

JEREMY: We were there to kill her, which we did.
               Tom held her down and I strangled her.

DSI JOHNS: Sorry? I mean… (Inaudible) Did you say
               you killed Mrs. Lavalier?

JEREMY: Yeah. Tom and I did, that is. Isn't that
               why you want me here?

               (Inaudible)

DSI JOHNS: You intend to confess now, to the killing?

JEREMY: Yeah. And about Giles Botnitch and
               Stanley Amis, too.

DSI JOHNS: Wait a minute, you killed them too?

Jeremy： 一個小時左右。

DSI Johns： 那之後你去了哪裡？

Jeremy： 之後我和 Tom 去了考菲爾德街探望
Lavalier 太太。

DSI Johns： 會見 Lavalier 夫人的目的是甚麼？

Jeremy： 我們想把她殺了，而且我們達成目的
了。Tom 按住她，我勒死了她。

DSI Johns： 甚麼？我是指⋯⋯（聽不清楚）你説你們
殺了 Lavalier 太太？

Jeremy： 對啊。我和 Tom 殺掉她了，就是這樣。
這不是你們找我來這裡的原因嗎？

（聽不清楚）

DSI Johns： 你現在是打算承認殺人嗎？

Jeremy： 是啊，還有 Giles Botnitch 和 Stanley
Amis。

DSI Johns： 等等，你把他們也殺了？

JEREMY: Yeah. Again, with Tom.

DSI JOHNS: Well... then...

               (Inaudible)

JEREMY: You don't recognise me, do you, DSI
               Johns?

DSI JOHNS: No.

JEREMY: You live on Fleeter Street, right? That
               nice house with a little stone arch in the
               front.

DSI JOHNS: Uh...

JEREMY: Well, I've delivered pizzas to your house,
               I don't know, fifty times maybe. It's
               always the same order: One Large Super
               Supreme, Garlic Bread and a bottle of
               Pepsi.

DSI JOHNS: Look...

Jeremy： 是的。也是和 Tom 一起。

DSI Johns： 嗯⋯⋯那麼⋯⋯

（聽不清楚）

Jeremy： 你不認得我嗎，Johns 長官？

DSI Johns： 不認得。

Jeremy： 你住在弗利特街，對吧？門口有個小石拱門的那座漂亮房子。

DSI Johns： 呃⋯⋯

Jeremy： 我送薄餅到你家已經⋯⋯我記不清楚，可能有五十次了吧？總是一樣的訂單，一個超級至尊大批、蒜蓉包和一支百事可樂。

DSI Johns： 等一下⋯⋯

JEREMY:	You live with your pretty wife, Jan, I think her name is, and two daughters, Elaine and Kelly. Am I right? You've got to be one of our most steady customers. Same order, at the same time every week, except maybe around holidays.
DSI JOHNS:	Where is your friend Tom? Where is he?
	(Banging and scraping noise? otherwise inaudible.)
JEREMY:	(Voice sounds strained) And every Tuesday at 6:30, to the minute. I reckon that's the only time of the day when the whole family can get together. The only time of the week when you're all together at the house and you eat a cheap pizza. Sad really.
DSI JOHNS:	(Screaming, heavy breathing.) Where is Tom?

END TRANSCRIPT.

Jeremy：	你和漂亮的妻子一起住，她的名字好像是叫 Jan 吧，還有兩個叫 Elaine 和 Kelly 的女兒。我有說對嗎？你是我們最固定的客戶之一，除了在假期前後可能不準時，其餘日子都是每個星期、相同時間，點一樣的東西。

DSI Johns： 你的朋友 Tom 呢？他在哪裡？

（敲打和刮擦的聲音？不然聽不清楚。）

Jeremy： （聲音聽起來很緊張）逢星期二，六點半，非常準時。我估計那是一天之中唯一可以全家人聚首一堂的時間，一週之中唯一可以安坐家中一起吃便宜薄餅的寶貴時刻。真叫人難過。

DSI Johns： （尖叫，呼吸急促）Tom 在哪裡？

逐字稿完結。

I'm Thankful for... The Women that Come in When Momma's at Work!

"I'm thankful for... the women that come in when Momma's at work!" Sofie said upon being called on to share her thankfulness at Ms. Bernard's 2nd grade Thanksgiving party.

Ms. Bernard, mildly concerned, pressed further. "Why are you thankful for them, Sofie?"

"Cause when they come in, my big brother takes me to get ice cream from DQ."

With that, the little girl adjusted her construction-paper pilgrim hat and resumed eating her pizza.

Now, Ms. Bernard didn't want to pry into the life of one of her students, and there could always have been a different explanation for the many women frequenting Sofie's home. However, considering Sofie's dad tried to pick up Ms. Bernard at their first parent-teacher conference, she decided that intervention was necessary.

She decided to soften the confrontation with homemade mashed potatoes. It was her grandmother-from-Idaho's recipe, so it was delicious.

我很感激那些姨姨

「我很感激……那些在媽媽上班時，來我們家的姨姨們！」Sofie 在 Bernard 老師的二年級感恩節聚會上，獲邀分享她感恩的事。

Bernard 老師有點擔心，進一步追問：「為甚麼要感謝她們呢，Sofie？」

「因為姨姨們過來時，我大哥就會帶我去 Dairy Queen 買雪糕。」

說罷，小女孩戴好頭上那頂用圖畫紙摺成、感恩節必備的朝聖者帽子，繼續吃著薄餅。

本來 Bernard 老師並不想八卦學生的私生活，而且那些女性經常到 Sofie 家，可以有很多不同的原因，但考慮到第一次家長會時，Sofie 的爸爸試圖跟 Bernard 老師搭訕調情，她認為必須干預這件事。

Bernard 老師決定帶上自製薯蓉來緩和衝突。這是她來自愛達荷州的祖母所傳授的食譜，很好吃的。

When she walked up to the home and rang the doorbell, she was surprised to find her 7-year-old student answering the door.

"Ms. Bernard! What're you doing here? We don't have school this week."

"Hey, Sofie. Is your dad home, sweetie?"

"Oh, did you come to see him? He's not here right now, but you can come upstairs and we can have a tea party!"

Ms. Bernard didn't want to go in, though she loved tea parties, and violated their privacy.

But, she didn't want to leave and come back later even more though, so she set her potatoes on the counter and walked up the stairs.

After maybe 10 minutes of tea-partying, with real-but-terrible tea, might she add, she heard Sofie's dad call for his kids.

When she and Sofie came down the stairs, Nolan, the 17-year-old brother, quickly glanced from the teacher to his father, grabbed his keys, and gestured for Sofie to walk with him out the door.

Bernard 老師走到一間房子，按響門鈴，她那七歲的學生應了門，這使她很驚訝。

「Bernard 老師！你怎麼來了？我們這個星期沒有課啊？」

「嗨，Sofie，親愛的，你爸爸在家嗎？」

「哦，你是來找他的嗎？他現在不在家，不過你可以先上來坐坐，我們可以一起喝下午茶！」

雖然 Bernard 老師喜歡下午茶，但她不想進去打擾他們一家。

不過，她更不想離開後再回來，所以她把薯蓉放在櫃檯上，然後走上了樓梯。

下午茶時段大概只過了十分鐘，Bernard 老師在心裡嘀咕著那些茶實在難以入口，然後她聽到 Sofie 的爸爸在呼喚孩子。

當她和 Sofie 一起走到樓下時，十七歲的哥哥 Nolan 的目光迅速從老師身上移到爸爸身上，快飛地拿了爸爸的鑰匙，然後示意 Sofie 和他一起出門走走。

When the two were gone, Ms. Bernard started with, "Mr. Stanton, in class a few days ago, Sofie said something that made me slightly worried about her home life."

She turned to face the man.

"I'm worried that the women she's seeing come in and out of the house will have a negative impact on her feelings toward the role of a woman in the future, and adultery is a fast-track to divorce, which has even worse impacts on a child's —"

She faltered, and started getting woozy.

"Tea party, huh?" Mr. Stanton said as Ms. Bernard sat on the couch. "Giving Sofie my Rohypnol to use as sugar was such a great idea."

"What?" Ms. Bernard slurred.

"She does good work. 'The good sugar is for guests only,' I say. She's very polite, isn't she? And, drugging 'em all with her tea makes my work easier."

At this point, he'd hoisted her up and was bringing her to the basement door.

兩人離開後，Bernard 老師首先開口：「Stanton 先生，幾天前在課堂上，Sofie 説了一句話，讓我有點擔心她的家庭生活。」

她轉身面向 Stanton 先生。

「我擔心 Sofie 看到那些頻繁進出你家的女人，會對她未來對女性角色的看法產生負面影響，而且通姦很容易導致離婚，更加影響孩子的……」

她支吾起來，開始頭暈目眩。

「來喝下午茶喔？」Stanton 先生説道，Bernard 老師則坐到沙發上。「把我的安眠藥給 Sofie 當作砂糖使用真是個好主意呢。」

「甚麼？」Bernard 老師口齒不清。

「她做得很好，因為我説『優質砂糖只可以給客人享用』。她很有教養，對吧？而且利用她的茶給你們下藥，讓我的工作更輕鬆了呢。」

這時，Stanton 先生已經把 Bernard 老師抱起來，來到了地下室門口。

"Man. It sucks that you brought your own car. Now I've gotta figure out how to get rid of it."

Suddenly producing a knife, maybe from his belt or the counter, he sliced her throat open and tossed her down the stairs into the basement.

She felt the wooden boards leave splinters in her skin as she tumbled, her own hot blood saturating her clothing as it spilled out.

By the time she'd landed with a dull thud on the concrete, she couldn't feel the pain of the fall anymore.

"And hey," he called to the near-lifeless teacher. "Thanks for the potatoes."

"These'll be perfect for Thanksgiving."

「哎，不好了，你怎麼開了自己的車來……那我就要想辦法弄走它啊。」

不知是從腰帶或是櫃檯拿來，Stanton 先生猛然拿出了刀，割破了 Bernard 老師的喉嚨，然後把她扔進了樓下的地下室。

滾下樓梯的同時，她感覺到地板的木刺扎進了她的皮膚，溫熱的鮮血湧出，浸濕了她的衣服。

她落在水泥地上，發出一聲悶響。此時的她已經感覺不到墜落的疼痛。

「嘿，」他對奄奄一息的老師喊道，「謝謝你的薯蓉喔。」

「這些都是感恩節的完美搭配。」

I Stared into Eyes that Weren't Hers

The metronome of the old clock hanging in our kitchen was all that broke the silence. Not so much as a sound could be heard from outside. Living in the woods, quiet nights were not only a rarity but damn near an impossibility. Yet here we were, not even a cricket or gust of wind through the heavy evergreen canopy. In the air I could almost feel a current, as if someone was running a battery in the space between me and the door.

I stood at the foot of our stairs. Was sound asleep only about twenty minutes ago but God that felt like an eternity now. Fast asleep I heard something, almost thought it was part of a dream. Someone was tinkering with the door, trying to get inside. I thought that maybe my wife had left behind her keys like she sometimes does. A nurse at the town hospital about an hour drive away. Graveyard shift, we're both not fans but she had to start somewhere. She'd left a couple of hours ago and it was still dead of night so there shouldn't be a reason why she'd be back so soon. Yet here we were, staring at each other with about fifteen feet of distance and our front door separating us.

Something was wrong, not just the situation which was catastrophically bad but something else. Our front door was a simple wooden structure with a small window in the top center and a thin curtain hanging over it. I saw my wife's

我凝視那雙不屬於她的眼睛

掛在廚房那個舊鐘的節拍器打破了寂靜，外面卻半點聲音都聽不見。住在樹林裡，安靜的夜晚不僅很少見，而且幾乎是不可能的。可是現在，聽不見蟋蟀的唧唧聲，也沒有風吹過那些厚重的常綠樹冠的沙沙聲。我彷彿感到空氣中有股電流，就好像有人在我和門之間的空間用電池那樣。

我站在樓梯口。我大約二十分鐘前才剛睡著，但是天啊，現在感覺好像過了一輩子那麼久。熟睡的我聽見了一些聲音，差點以為是夢裡的聲響。有人想進來，所以在擺弄門。我猜想是妻子忘了帶鑰匙，她有時也會這樣。她是個護士，在大約一個小時車程以外的市立醫院上班。她要值大夜班，雖然我們都不喜歡夜班，但她始終要開展護士生涯，只好硬著頭皮。她幾個小時前就出門了，現在還是夜深人靜，所以她應該不會這麼快回來。但現在她就站在門前，和我隔著大約十五英呎的距離，凝視著彼此，中間只隔著一道門。

有些不妥。情況不僅是災難級般糟糕，還有更可怕的事。我們的前門是道簡潔的木門，上方中央有一扇小窗戶，上面掛著薄薄的窗簾。我透過窗戶看到妻子的臉，但凝視著我的不是妻子。我很了解她的眼神。在我們一起生活的歲月裡，我常常看著她的雙眼，然後不自覺地沉醉在裡面。即使在黑暗中，我也能一眼認出她溫柔而慈愛的目光。但在我眼前的，

face looking at me through the window but what stared back at me was not my wife. I knew her eyes. I'd stared into them and lived lifetimes getting lost in them in our years together. Even in the dark, I knew her soft, loving gaze anywhere. This was a cold stare, no sign of emotion whatsoever. These eyes belonged to something more beast than man, certainly not a woman. The door knob shuffled again. Whoever this imposter was, *it* wanted inside. I took a slow step forward and saw *it* vanish as *it* wandered around the house looking for a way in. I found my gun safe and unlocked it. A 44 Magnum Revolver awaited anyone who wanted to test me tonight.

I went around the home and checked all the windows and doors and secured *it*. Occasionally, I looked out and caught a glimpse of the thing outside, stalking me from just out of view. Our game of hide and seek continued until morning. Light came and that's when I finally saw *it* wander off into the treeline. I called the police and told them to be on their way. They arrived and I greeted them at the front door. The smell hit me before the sight, I looked down and saw her. Not even ten feet from our front door, still in her scrubs sitting in the grass. There was a pool of blood around her head, with flesh peeled from her neck up. Right down to her bare skull.

是冰冷的目光，不帶任何情緒。這雙眼睛屬於比人更有獸性的東西，肯定不是個女人。門把又被扭動了。不管這個假冒者是誰，*牠*就是想要進來。我緩緩踏前了一步，*牠*正圍著屋子四周遊蕩，想找地方闖進來，所以不再停在門前。我找到了放槍的夾萬，然後打開了它。我那把 44 萬能左輪手槍，等待著這晚的挑戰者。

我在家裡四處走動，檢查所有門窗並把它們上鎖。偶爾望向外面，會瞥見外面的那個傢伙，*牠*也一直在盯著屋內的我。我們的捉迷藏遊戲一直持續到早上。天亮了，那時我終於看到*牠*溜進了樹林。我馬上報警，拜託他們趕快過來。他們到了，我在前門迎接他們。一股氣味撲面而來，我低頭就看到了她。離前門不到十英呎的距離，她仍然穿著工作服坐在草地上。她頭部周圍有一大灘血，脖子上的肉都被剝掉了，一直到頭骨都是光禿禿的。

I Love My Mommy

I really do. My mommy is the best mommy in the world! She found me when I was very little and gave me a whole lot of love, and now I'm so big! I'm not as big as mommy's other babies, but that's ok. She's had longer to love them. And maybe someday I'll be that big from all the love mommy gives me.

Mommy's other babies don't come to see her very often anymore. I think this makes mommy sad, but I try to help. I snuggle in her lap and purr as loud as I can, so mommy will know how much I love her.

It's been a long time since any of mommy's other babies came to see her, and she is so sad about it. Even with my best purrs and snuggles, I can't make her feel better. And she's been so tired lately. But that's ok. Mommy can sleep as much as she wants. I know she still loves me.

Mommy was sad again today. All day. But that's ok. I gave her all the love I could. Tonight, when we went to bed, I snuggled up right next to her and purred until we both fell asleep. I think that's good. Mommy is still so tired and needs a good sleep.

Mommy didn't wake up this morning. She must be so, so, so tired. That's ok. I still have some food in my bowl from last night. I'll be ok until she wakes up later.

我很愛媽媽

我真的很愛她。我媽媽是世界上最好的媽媽！她在我還很小的時候找到了我，給我滿滿的愛，現在我已經長大了！我沒有媽媽的其他寶寶那麼大，但不要緊，她有更多時間去愛他們。也許有一天我也會因為媽媽給我的愛而長得那麼大。

媽媽的其他寶寶不再經常來看她了。媽媽很難過，但我會盡力幫助她。我依偎在她的膝上，盡我所能地大聲呼嚕著，讓媽媽知道我有多愛她。

媽媽的其他任何一個寶寶已經很久沒有來看她了，她很悲傷。即使我多麼努力呼嚕和依偎，都無法讓她心情轉好。而且她最近都很累。但沒關係，媽媽想睡多久就睡多久。我知道她還是很愛我。

媽媽今天也很傷心，一整天都很傷心。但沒關係，我給她我所有的愛。今晚我們上床睡覺時，我依偎在她身邊，不斷呼嚕，直到我們都睡著。我覺得這樣很好。媽媽還是很累，需要好好睡一覺。

媽媽今天早上沒有醒來，她一定是太累了。沒關係，我的碗裡還有昨晚的食物。在她待會醒來之前我不會餓著的。

Mommy didn't wake up all day today. I'm worried about her a lot. I'm gonna sleep next to her again and hopefully she'll be better in the morning.

It's been days and mommy still hasn't woken up. And worse, she's cold! I've tried everything I can to help her. I even tried yelling to wake her up, but I felt so bad about it after. I'm so worried. I hope one of mommy's other babies comes by soon. They'll know what to do.

Mommy still hasn't woken up. And I'm getting tired too. Her other babies never came. I think I'll lay down next to mommy and we can both take a long sleep together.

媽媽一整天都沒有醒來。我很擔心她，我會再次睡在她身邊，希望她明天早上會好些吧。

已經好幾天了，媽媽還沒睡醒。更糟糕的是，她很冷！我已盡我所能幫助她，我甚至試過大吼大喊叫醒她，但之後我覺得這樣不好。我好擔心。我很希望媽媽的其他寶寶有誰會快點過來，他們會知道該怎麼做。

媽媽還沒醒過來，我也開始累了。她其他寶寶也沒有來過。我只好躺在媽媽旁邊，一起睡個大覺。

The Pendant

"Fifty bucks and it's yours." the dirty cheap jewelry peddling stall owner said. "I saw you eyeing it for a while now, I know you want it," he said, smirking with what was left of his blackened, rotting teeth.

My head was spinning, I wanted to cry, to scream, to shout, to grab the dirty old peddler by the neck, but all I was able to do was stare blankly at the unique white gold pendant with a rose, engraved with the initials M. J. F. in it.

"C'mon buddy, I haven't got all day, I said fifty or move it." the old man yelled, as I was still comprehending, why the pendant my father and I had made for my mum, who passed away two years prior and was buried with it, was on this dirty old sales table.

吊墜

「五十塊就有交易囉。」賣骯髒廉價的珠寶攤檔老闆說：「我看你盯著它好一會了，我知道你很想把它帶回家喔。」他假笑著說，露出嘴裡所剩無幾、發黑腐爛的牙齒。

我覺得天旋地轉，我想哭，想尖叫，想怒罵，想扼住那個髒兮兮老小販的脖子，但我只能呆呆地瞪著那個獨特的白金玫瑰吊墜，上面刻著簡寫 M. J. F.。

「快點啦，我沒有一整天跟你耗，五十塊，不然就滾開。」老人喊道，而我還在深思，為何父親和我親手為兩年前去世的母親製作、連同母親一同下葬的吊墜，會出現在這個骯髒破舊的攤檔裡。

Fool Me Thrice

"Ugh." It's 3 am. That horrible siren has started up again. I'm up for a pee. I'm not remotely awake. "F**k." It's piercing. "Gerard!" I call out. Wipe. Flush. Head to the bedroom. "GERARD!" F**k that man sleeps like the dead. I have to kick the bed before he even starts to rustle. I don't even have to say anything. He hears it.

"Not again…" he moans tiredly. "Cynthia?"

"Yeah, I'm on it."

I'm wearing PJ's. The kind with pants. Normally I'd throw on some jeans and a t-shirt just in case, but this is what… the fourth time in a couple of weeks? I'm clothed enough.

I grab a tote off the fridge and start chucking. Pills. Wallets. Small valuables. Gerard will get his computer. I should get mine.

We don't have kids or pets, thankfully.

"Got everything?" he asks, holding his laptop under one arm.

"No," I scoff tiredly. "Let's get this over with."

狼來了

「呃……」現在是凌晨三點，那嚇人的警報又響了。我起床上廁所，但還未完全清醒。「媽的。」很刺耳啊。「Gerard！」我呼喚。擦拭，沖洗，前往睡房。「Gerard！！！」那個男人他媽的睡得像死屍一樣。在他發脾氣之前，我已經踢了一下床。我甚至不用開口，他都聽見了。

「又來……」他疲倦地抱怨著：「Cynthia？」

「知道了，我去處理。」

我穿著睡衣，有褲子的那款。通常我會換上牛仔褲和 T 袖以防萬一，但這已經是……幾星期內第四次了？我這樣的裝束可以了。

我拿了掛在冰箱的手提袋，把所有東西丟進去：藥品、錢包、小件的貴重物品。Gerard 會拿他的電腦，我也要拿我的。

感恩我們沒有孩子或寵物。

「東西都拿好了嗎？」把手提電腦夾在腋下的他問道。

「沒有，」我疲倦地嘲笑道：「快點結束這件事吧。」

Another night with another alarm and a meeting of the building's collective minds.

We leave the apartment, and I pause to knock on our neighbour's door. She's old. Someone's grandmother. She's kind of mean, but I feel a duty there. So I knock. Knock again. Gerard's locked our door and is trying to hustle me along now. That alarm is still blaring, and now that I'm fully awake, it makes me nervous. It always makes me nervous.

"Come on," he urges, and we walk away. Open the hallway doors. They slam shut the moment the alarm starts blaring. Don't take the elevator; it's not 'safe'. So we join the parade in the stairwell. Not as many people this time. Fool me thrice, I guess.

We file outside, and I'm feeling foolish for not grabbing a sweater. It's always chilly in the wee hours.

Everyone's chatting and wondering who set it off this time. Who is tonight's sh*tty cook? Who set the dryer on fire? Some of us are laughing until the first person spots the smoke. Then a lick of flame, lapping in and out of view. All laughter stops, and the murmuring begins.

又一個響警報的夜晚，整棟大廈的人都聚集起來。

我們離開住所，經過鄰居家時我停了下來敲敲她的門。她是個老婆婆，某人的祖母。雖然她有點刻薄，但我覺得自己有責任提醒她，所以我敲了門，敲了好幾次。此時 Gerard 鎖好了我們家的門，然後催促我快點走。警報還在響，讓現在完全清醒的我很緊張。我每次都很緊張。

「走吧。」他催促道，接著我們就離開了。我們打開走廊的門，在警報響起的那一刻猛然關上。不要乘坐電梯，因為不「安全」。所以我們加入了走樓梯的人群。這次不算很多人，可能覺得是「狼來了」。

我們在大廈外面排隊等候，沒穿毛衣的我覺得自己很笨，因為凌晨時份總是很冷。

大家議論紛紛，討論著今次是誰觸發警報。誰是今晚的地獄廚神？誰的乾衣機著火了？我們有些人笑個不停，直至有人發現了煙霧，然後更冒出了一團忽隱忽現的火焰。再沒有人在笑，換來的是竊竊私語。

The sounds of a fire truck can be heard in the distance, but right here, right now, we hear glass shattering as the roar of fire quickly grows and consumes. A shout as someone tries to climb out from their patio. We see faces in the windows, hear screams. I turn away and realize that the sound of sobbing is coming from me. I'm not cold anymore.

消防車的聲音從遠處傳來，但就在此時此刻此地，我們聽見玻璃碎裂的聲音，火勢迅速蔓延，吞噬著一切。有人邊從露台裡爬出來邊大叫著。我們看見了窗邊的一些面孔，聽見了尖叫聲。我別過臉，才意識到抽泣聲是從自己身上傳來的。我不再覺得冷了。

If Everyone Gave a Single Penny

That was it, the last straw.

Mitch was the owner and chief of operations for a widely used internet encyclopedia. Billions of bits of information safely stored and made readily available for all to see at the click of a button. For years, he had shouldered nearly the entire expensive cost of the service. Public donations provided some small relief, but this most recent quarter yielded the lowest returns yet. Mitch would be out of pocket nearly 3/4 of the increasing cost of running this platform, and years of a worsening problem finally caught up to him.

Big flashing letters atop the site reads the news.

"ONE MILLION DOLLARS TO BE RAISED BY THE PUBLIC!"

The challenge was given to the users of the site. They were given 30 days, starting the following Monday. In that time, the site easily reached a hundred million people. If everyone gave a single penny, they'd reach the goal. If the goal was not met, Mitch made an agreement with a local demolition company to destroy the servers, and all would be lost. Decades of information and work down the drain in what was sure to be an epic explosion.

集腋成裘

這是最後一根稻草。

Mitch 是一家被廣泛使用的互聯網百科全書的擁有人和運營總監。網站安全地儲存了數十億個資訊，所有用戶只要點擊幾下就可以隨時查看。多年來，他幾乎承擔了這項服務的全數昂貴費用。公眾捐款只能略微緩解經濟壓力，但最近一個季度的回報率是迄今為止最低的。為了支付網站不斷增加的成本，Mitch 不惜自掏腰包至積蓄只剩四分之一，但多年來不斷惡化的問題終於讓他無力繳付費用。

網站頂部閃爍的大字顯示著一則消息：

「眾籌一百萬美元！」

那是給網站用戶的一個挑戰。從下星期一開始，他們有三十天的時間進行捐款。那陣子網站輕鬆就能達到了一億人次流量。如果每個人都捐一分錢，就能達成目標。Mitch 與當地一家拆遷公司達成協議，如果無法達成目標，拆遷公司就會銷毀伺服器，所有資料都會化為烏有。數十年以來儲存的資料和投放的心血，都會在史詩般的爆炸中付諸東流。

Mitch hoped such a challenge would inspire the selfish users of his site. There was no other database that came close to this one, at least not for free. People initially thought it was a prank and ignored it. Finally, after a week, the donations started coming in. They'd raised about $100,000 the following week, and money started rolling in at a decent pace. At least until the final five-day count.

At the top of the final five days, ananonymous billionaire donated just enough money to bring the grand total up to $999,999. Mitch was ecstatic, to say the least, and started a celebration in his office. There was no way that the millions of people using the site couldn't donate a single dollar over the next five days. Turns out, that was exactly what everyone else thought as well. For the next couple of days, the number didn't budge. Everyone was so sure that someone would cover the last dollar, a single dollar, that no one bothered to do it themselves. Then came the final day, the final hour, the final minutes and still the donation total remained the same.

Mitch had been so sure that he'd stopped keeping track of the counter, knowing for sure it must be miles above of the goal. With seconds to go, he turned on the timer to celebrate, and his heart sank.

Mitch 希望這個挑戰能激勵網站那些自私的用戶。沒有其他數據庫可以媲美這個數據庫，至少其他不是免費的。人們最初認為這是場惡作劇，所以沒有多加理會。終於在挑戰開始一星期後，人們紛紛開始捐款。在接下來的一星期，籌集了大約 100,000 美元，資金開始以可觀的速度流入。至少在挑戰最後五天之前也是如此。

在倒數五天時，一位匿名的億萬富翁捐了一筆錢，使捐款總額剛剛好達到 999,999 美元。Mitch 欣喜若狂，在辦公室裡開始慶祝。網站座擁數百萬個用戶，不可能在接下來的五天內捐不到 1 美元。但事實證明，每個人也是這樣想的。過了幾天，捐款數字紋風不動。每個人也覺得肯定會有人捐出那最後一美元，所以自己也不需費心捐款。然後到了最後一天、最後一小時、最後幾分鐘，捐款總數仍然維持不變。

Mitch 非常放心，所以他已經沒有盯著計時器，因為他知道捐款肯定會遠遠超過原定目標。只剩幾秒鐘，Mitch 打開計時器頁面準備慶祝時，他的心沉了下去。

Three.
Two.
One.

Everything Mitch had worked his life for was on a timer to go up in about fifteen minutes. Plenty of time to leave his office on the 20th floor but as he reached for his keys the will to escape left him. Instead, he leaned back in his recliner and waited for the ground to give out from beneath him in a fireball.

三。

二。

一。

Mitch 一生為之奮鬥的心血將會在十五分鐘後化為灰燼。他本來有足夠的時間離開位於二十樓的辦公室，但當他伸手去拿鑰匙時，逃跑的念頭一閃即逝。相反，他挨後靠在躺椅上，等待火球從地面冒出來吞噬自己。

"I'm Sorry to Say, It's in Stage 4."

The doctor's words rang out in my head, bounced from synapse to synapse, not capable of taking hold of a thought.

"We'll get you into chemotherapy right away. Since it's spread, an operation will only remove the tumors, but chemo will be necessary." the doctor said. I thanked him and left for home.

On my way home, my mind was full of thoughts. How could this have happened to me? To me, a person who never smoked, rarely drank alcohol, never took drugs and was a semi-professional athlete. Why me? What's gonna happen to my family? I couldn't find any answers, even as I entered my family's apartment.

I was instantly greeted by my 10-year-old son "Hey, dad, a package arrived for you. So, what did the doc say?" I couldn't bring myself to tell him the truth just yet. "A couple of things. Is mom feeling any better?" My wife has been feeling under the weather for some time, but recently she's been getting worse. She was stubborn as hell and refused to see the doctor, always blaming "female troubles" and the weather for her problems.

"She's sleeping right now. I'll go to Tommy's to study for the test if it's alright?" my son replied. "Sure, then we'll talk in the evening" I said, and my son was out the door.

「很抱歉，你已是末期。」

醫生的話在我腦中迴盪，在每個神經突觸裡不斷跳來跳去，使我無法定下來好好思考。

「要馬上給你做化療，因為它擴散了，手術只能切除腫瘤，但化療是必須的。」醫生說。我謝過他就回家了。

在回家的路上，我滿腦子都是疑問，這些事怎麼會發生在我身上？我是個從不抽煙、很少喝酒、從不吸毒的人，並且是個半職業運動員，為甚麼是我？我的家人會怎樣？甚至在我回到家的時候，我仍然找不到任何答案。

我十歲的兒子馬上跑來迎接我：「嘿，爸爸，你有包裹。還有，醫生怎麼說？」我還未準備好告訴他真相。「有說了幾件事。媽媽好點了嗎？」妻子身體抱恙已經有好一段時間了，但最近她的情況越來越嚴重。她固執得要死，不肯去看醫生，總是把問題歸咎於「女人的煩惱」和天氣。

「她睡著了，我想去 Tommy 家溫習，可以嗎？」兒子回答。「好的，那我們晚上再談。」我說罷，兒子就出門了。

I checked on my wife, asleep in bed. Then I grabbed the package that had arrived. I noticed it was probably about the faulty research equipment I had sent back to the manufacturer quite some time ago.

I retreated to my study and opened the package. I was first greeted by a letter. I opened it, read it, and dropped it in shock. It all made sense now. We're dead. I'm dead, my wife's dead, my son's dead.

The letter read: Greetings. We have reviewed your complaint about the faulty Geiger counter. We have tested said Geiger counter repeatedly, with several different test samples, and the readings were consistently within the stated error threshold. We would advise you to contact the Bureau of Nuclear Safety immediately, as your claims of the device giving a consistent false reading, consistently reading off the chart, seem to denote a heavy contamination in the area where you tested the Geiger counter.

I had tested it in our apartment. I never brought it anywhere else.

我查看了躺在床上睡著的妻子。然後我拿了送來的包裹。這應該是我很久之前寄回給製造商那個有瑕疵的研究設備。

我回到書房,打開包裹。先是一封信,我打開來閱讀它,然後震驚地把它扔掉了。現在一切都說得通了。我們死定了。我要死了,妻子要死了,兒子要死了。

信中寫道:您好,我們已經審查了您對蓋格計數器的故障投訴。我們用幾個不同的測試樣本對您的蓋格計數器進行了反覆測試,讀數沒有超出規定的誤差值。我們建議您立即與核安全局聯絡,因為您聲稱計數器一直顯示錯誤讀數,而且讀數持續高企,似乎表明您用蓋格計數器測試的區域受到嚴重污染。

我是在家裡測試的,從來沒有把它帶到其他任何地方。

TikTok Murder

New York Times, 2025, May 14:

"A Well Known TikTok Star, Melanee, Found Dead In Her Home"

Washington Post, 2025, July 12:

"Another TikTok Celebrity Found Dead, Fifth Prominent TikTok Personality To Be Killed, Authority Now Calling It Serial Murder"

New York Post, 2025, September 6:

"22 TikToker Stars Now Dead, Police No Closer To Catching The Killer"

Daily News, 2025, October 2:

"Police Believe Multiple Killers in TikTok Murders"

Arizona Sun, 2025, December 24:

"Google AI Suspected In Locating TikTok Murder Victims - Video Image Location Identification (VILI) algorithm may have been used by the killers"

Chicago Tribune, 2026, January 30:

"Column - How Google AI designed to locate terror cells are now being used to terrorize the teenagers of TikTok."

Dallas Caller, 2026, March 15:

"TikTok Killer Caught! He Says 'I'm not the only one. We're legion"

TikTok 殺人事件

《紐約時報》2025 年 5 月 14 日：

「知名 TikTok 明星 Melanee 在家中身亡」

《華盛頓郵報》2025 年 7 月 12 日：

「再有 TikTok 名人死亡，累計第五名 TikTok 名人被殺，當局視為連環謀殺案」

《紐約郵報》2025 年 9 月 6 日：

「共 22 名 TikTok 明星死亡，警方仍對兇手毫無頭緒」

《每日新聞》2025 年 10 月 2 日：

「警方相信 TikTok 謀殺案有多名兇手」

《亞利桑那太陽報》2025 年 12 月 24 日：

「兇手可能運用 Google 人工智能『影片圖像位置識別演算法』找出 TikTok 受害者位置」

《芝加哥論壇報》2026 年 1 月 30 日：

「專欄——旨在定位恐怖組織的 Google 人工智能，現反被用來恐嚇 TikTok 的青少年用戶」

《達拉斯傳訊》2026 年 3 月 15 日：

「TikTok 殺手落網！他表示『我不是單獨行事，我們是個軍團』」

Indiana Chronicle, 2026, April 5:

"TikTok Murder Toll Reaches 109. Authority Advising Users To Stop Streaming"

Savannah Mail, 2026, May 22:

"Column - My daughter streamed from a darkened and completely empty room so she couldn't be located. She was killed last month."

LA Times, 2026, June 23:

"TikTok Banned"

New York Times, 2026, July 9:

"Instagram Megastar Amilla Found Dead, TikTok Killers Suspected."

Boston Chronicles, 2026 October 3:

"9 Instagram Celebrities Dead, Authority Almost Certain TikTok Murder Continuing"

Cincinnati Bugle, 2026 December 15:

"68 Instagrammed Murdered This Month, Calls Grow To Ban All Streaming"

Miami Sun, 2027 February 2:

"2 More TikTok Killers Caught, They Say Hundreds Like Them"

《印第安納紀事報》2026 年 4 月 5 日：

「TikTok 謀殺案死亡人數增至 109 人；當局建議用戶停止直播」

《薩凡納郵報》2026 年 5 月 22 日：

「專欄──我女兒在一個又暗又空蕩的房間直播，理應無法定位她的位置。但她上個月被殺了。」

《洛杉磯時報》2026 年 6 月 23 日：

「全國禁用 TikTok」

《紐約時報》2026 年 7 月 9 日：

「Instagram 巨星 Amilla 身亡，懷疑 TikTok 殺手作案」

《波士頓紀事報》2026 年 10 月 3 日：

「9 名 Instagram 名人死亡，當局幾近肯定 TikTok 殺手仍然活躍」

《辛辛那提軍號報》2026 年 12 月 15 日：

「本月有 68 人在 Instagram 上被殺，禁止所有串流媒體的呼聲越來越高」

《邁阿密太陽報》2027 年 2 月 2 日：

「再多 2 名 TikTok 殺手被捕，聲稱有數百名支持者」

Oakland News, 2027 May 15:

"Instagram Banned, Authorities Considering Banning All Live Streaming"

Washington Post, 2027 June 20:

"Mass Protest At Against Live Streaming Ban, Organisers Call TikTok Murder a Hoax"

Baltimore Times, 2027 July 1:

"Column - No more live streaming? Are we back to blogging now like in 2003?"

New York Post, 2027 December 24:

"Meta Files For Bankruptcy, Zuckerberg Says Market Hostile To Social Media"

LA Sun Times, 2028 February 12:

"12 Girls Found Murdered In One House, No Links To Social Media"

New York Times, 2028 April 18:

"Times Square Digital Display Board Briefly Hijacked To Play A Scene From TV Show 'The Following'."

Detroit Daily, 2028 May 11:

"320 Teenage Girls Murdered Nationwide In The Past Month, Authorities Fear A Large Active Murder Cult."

《奧克蘭新聞》2027 年 5 月 15 日：

「全國禁用 Instagram，當局考慮禁止所有直播」

《華盛頓郵報》2027 年 6 月 20 日：

「直播禁令引發大規模示威抗議，組織者稱 TikTok 謀殺是一場騙局」

《巴爾的摩時報》2027 年 7 月 1 日：

「專欄——不再直播？我們會像 2003 年般回到部落格嗎？」

《紐約郵報》2027 年 12 月 24 日：

「Meta 申請破產，朱克伯格表示市場對社交媒體懷有敵意」

《洛杉磯太陽時報》2028 年 2 月 12 日：

「12 名女孩在同一所房子被殺，並無使用社交媒體」

《紐約時報》2028 年 4 月 18 日：

「時代廣場螢幕被短暫劫持，播放電視劇《門屠》」

《底特律日報》2028 年 5 月 11 日：

「上月全國有多達 320 名少女被謀殺，當局擔心會出現大規模的謀殺邪教。」

Intoxicated Delusion
醉 生 夢 死

My Husband Hasn't Spoken to Me for Days.

He sat still at the end of the table. His droopy eyes, rimmed with dark circles, reflected the dim lights of the dingy dining room.

Another failed gig, no doubt.

My friends had warned me about marrying him. Jason was a struggling artist, you see. "Don't settle for that man," They said, "You'll be broke your whole life."

Yet, when he got down on one knee and proposed with sincere eyes, I vowed that I would be by his side through thick and thin. When Jason finally reached his dreams, I would be there to celebrate with him.

We always prayed for a breakthrough, but failure after failure happened and five years together brought us to this dilapidated apartment.

My head throbbed. Jason's tiredness must be rubbing off on me.

"Honey," I whispered reassuringly, "I'll always be with you no matter what, and I'm sure that everything will get better soon."

He didn't reply, dull eyes staring into nothing.

老公不再跟我說話了

他一動不動地坐在桌子的一端。黑眼圈框著他下垂的雙眼，跟陰暗骯髒飯廳的微弱燈光互相輝映。

肯定又是一場失敗的演出。

朋友警告過我不要嫁給他。看吧，Jason 是個在掙扎求存的藝術家。「不要為了那個男人委屈自己，」他們說：「你一輩子都會捱窮的。」

然而，當他單膝跪地、用真誠的眼神向我求婚時，我發誓會與他同甘共苦。當 Jason 終於能實現夢想之時，我就會和他一起慶祝。

我們總是希望有所突破，但願望一次又一次的落空。相處五年的我們搬到了這間破舊的公寓。

我的頭陣陣作痛，似乎是被 Jason 的疲倦影響到了。

「親愛的，」我低聲地安慰說：「無論發生甚麼事，我都會在你身邊，我相信一切都會很快好起來的。」

他沒有回答，空洞的雙眼沒有焦點。

"I made something special," I said with a small smile, beef casserole in hand. "Go ahead and take a bite. I promise it's good."

He remained listless, not even lifting his fork. Minutes passed like that, and I felt a tear roll down my cheek as I rubbed my temple. Jason used to love my food. Even when I burnt everything when I just started learning how to cook, he'd beam at me and joke that he didn't deserve to eat food made by an angel.

Love, faith and hope had kept us together, but perhaps Jason had gotten tired. Would he give up on his dreams? Would he stop smiling forever?

Would he leave me?

My head felt like it was splitting open now. I hurriedly tried to make my way to the bathroom but tripped on the glass wine bottles littering the floor.

Jason must have heard the commotion, but he never came. As I lied there helplessly, writhing and clutching my head, I wondered when everything started spiraling.

Was it when he started drinking? Or was it when I told him that I wanted to work and support us?

「我煮了特別的餸菜,」手裡拿著砂鍋燉牛肉的我微笑著說:
「來吃一口吧,我保證好吃喔。」

他仍然無精打采,連叉子也沒有拿起。不知過了多少分鐘,
我邊揉著太陽穴,邊感覺到淚水順著臉頰滾落了下來。
Jason 以前很愛我煮的東西,那時候我剛開始學煮飯,把所
有東西都煮焦了,他也會開玩笑說他不配吃天使煮的食物。

愛、信任和希望維繫著我們,但也許 Jason 已經厭倦了。他
會放棄夢想嗎?他永遠都不會再笑了嗎?

他會離開我嗎?

我的頭感覺要裂開了。我急忙想跑去洗手間,卻被散落在地
上的玻璃酒瓶絆倒了。

Jason 一定聽到了這陣噪音,但他一直沒來查看。我無助地
抱著頭躺在地上打滾,天旋地轉。

是他開始喝酒的時候嗎?還是我告訴他我想找工作幫補家計
的時候?

Maybe it was when I told him that I was pregnant...

"A baby?" He shouted, as he held me by my hair after punching me in the gut, "In this f**king mess?"

I sobbed for what seemed like hours, until the pain subsided again into a dull throb. I got up shakily and walked to the mirror.

A monster stared back at me. Disgusting black ooze trickled down from a grotesque hole at the side of its face. It was pungent, smelling of *death*. Brain matter, dark and rotten, slipped through, making sickening squelches as it fell to the ground.

My mind whirred as I made my way back. Jason had not taken a single bite of the beef casserole, now rotten as if it has been left out for several days.

It wasn't tiredness or sadness in his eyes, I realised — It was guilt.

Guilt from killing me.

可能是我告訴他我懷孕了的時候吧⋯⋯

「寶寶？」他先是打了我肚子一拳，然後抓住我的頭髮大喊道：「你還嫌不夠煩嗎？」

我哭了很久，感覺像過了好幾個小時，直到劇痛再次消退，變回深沉的隱隱作痛。我顫抖著站起身，走到鏡子前。

鏡子裡的怪物回瞪著我。怪物臉頰上有一個奇形怪狀的洞，一些像爛泥般噁心的黑色物體從那裡滴落下來，味道很刺鼻，帶有死亡的氣息。深色且發臭的大腦物質徐徐滑落，掉到地上時發出令人不安的吱吱聲。

我走回去找 Jason，腦袋嗡嗡作響。那鍋燉牛肉 Jason 一口都沒有吃，似乎已經放了很多天而變壞了。

我才知道，他眼中的不是疲倦或悲傷——而是愧疚。

愧疚把我殺了。

You Should Think of Your Family Before You Try to Commit Suicide

I was assigned a patient within the last minute, and he had just tried to commit suicide. I knew nothing else about him. The first thing I said to him was to think about his family. I told him what his mother would think if he wasn't around and how distraught she would be if he was dead. The mother would be so traumatised especially being the person who gave birth to him. I told him how his mother would miss him and how all mothers cherish their children, and to put a mother through all of that would be devastating for her.

Then I said things about how his father would feel if he had committed suicide. His father would be broken, as fathers also love their children. I told him how his suicide would put tears to his father's eyes, and how he would not be able to see his bloodline move forward. His father would tremble because he would not have any grandchildren, and it would be such a lonely existence for the father. For both parents it would be such a loss as all that work and time would be a waste if he had committed suicide. I kept telling my patient to also think about how his friends would feel and even his coworkers.

Then I went a bit further and told him to think about his siblings and to understand how they would feel if he had committed suicide. Growing up together and then suddenly for everything to just go down the soil, it would be soul-crushing for them. I got a bit louder and told him whether

自殺前請想想你的家人

我準備下班之際，他們安排了一個病人給我。我只知道他剛剛試圖自殺，沒有更多資料。我對他說的第一件事就是勸他想想家人。我告訴他，如果他不再在母親身邊，她會怎麼想，如果他死了，她會多麼心煩意亂。母親身為生下他的人，會受到巨大的創傷。我告訴他，母親會多麼想念他，天下所有母親都非常愛惜自己的骨肉。要是母親痛失兒子，會徹底毀了她。

我接著說要是他自殺了，父親會怎麼想。深愛孩子的父親會心碎。我再跟他說，他自殺會讓父親流淚，他將無法看到血統傳承。父親會因為沒有孫子孫女而顫抖，這對父親來說會非常孤獨。如果他自殺了，對父母雙方來說都是一種損失，因為所有養育他的心思和時間都會浪費掉。我不斷告訴病人也要考慮朋友，甚至同事的感受。

我再說得深入點，叫他想想兄弟姊妹，想像如果他自殺了兄弟姐妹會有甚麼感受。大家一起長大，然後突然間一切都土崩瓦解，這對他們來說像是天塌下來。我提高聲量，問他會否認為兄弟姐妹在他自殺後仍然可以活得安好。我希望讓病人意識到如果他自殺會影響到多少人。在他離開之前，我一直敦促他要深思熟慮。

he would think his siblings would feel great after his suicide. I made my patient realise the amount of people it would affect if he was to commit suicide. I kept urging him to think before he left.

Then I told him to think how his grandparents would feel if he had committed suicide, and if he committed suicide, it would surely crush his grandparents. My patient had such a large family and his suicide would affect a lot of people including his cousins and uncles, I tried to make the patient realise the amount of damage his suicide will have on so many people, and then after giving that speech to my last minute patient, I opened the file and I was shocked at what i had learnt.

His whole family including his mother, father, siblings, grandparents and all the cousins had imprisoned and tortured him, and were preparing him for a satanic sacrifice. He tried to commit suicide to escape from being offered up to Satan. His neighbours phoned the police for strange noises coming from his house.

I then said to him "actually ignore what I said and don't think about your family."

It was too late. He grabbed one of my pens and stabbed himself in the neck.

然後我就叫他想想，如果他自殺了，爺爺嫲嫲會怎麼想。如果他自殺了，他爺爺嫲嫲肯定會崩潰的。這位病人來自一個大家庭，他自殺會影響到很多人，包括他的堂、表兄弟姊妹和叔叔阿姨。我試圖讓病人意識到他的自殺會對很多人造成傷害，然後在我給這名最後一位病人演說完之後，我打開文件夾，望著病人資料，震驚不已。

他的整個家族，包括他父母親、兄弟姊妹、爺爺嫲嫲、公公婆婆和所有堂、表兄弟姊妹，都曾經囚禁他、對他施暴，甚至準備犧牲他來進行惡魔獻祭。他因此自殺來逃避被奉獻給撒旦。他的鄰居聽見他家發出奇怪聲響而報警。

然後我就對他說：「其實別理我的話，別想著你的家人。」

可惜為時已晚，他已抓起了我的一支筆刺向自己的脖子。

The Last Will and Testament of William Opie

"This video recording was made by me, William Opie, and it is to be my final will regarding my estate. My lawyer, Philip Gill is currently present as my witness.

John, Simon and Bailey, my children, I trust Philip has brought you all to his office, as I instructed him, and you are now watching this video. You're all probably waiting eagerly to find out how much money you'll be receiving from my estate. I suspect you've been longing for this day for some time now.

Unfortunately, my children, I will not be giving you anything. Instead, I will be taking something from you today.

You see, one of... I mean, three of the greatest mistakes in my life were having you three kids. Sure, with each new birth, I was hopeful for having a wonderful child who'd enrich our lives. But you all turned out to be a terrible lot.

You are unkind, greedy, ungrateful, rude and generally vicious people. For many decades, you tormented your mother, Kim, and me so much, that we dreaded seeing you. Your abuses didn't end even in our old years, and I am quite convinced that it was you who sent Kim to her early grave.

Opie 先生的遺囑

「這段影片是我 William Opie 錄製的，會是關於我遺產的最終遺囑。我的律師 Philip Gill 正在現場當我的見證人。

John、Simon 和 Bailey，我的孩子們，我相信 Philip 已按照我的指示將你們帶到了他的辦公室，而你們現在正觀看這段影片。你們應該急不及待很想知道我會分多少錢給你們，我在想，你們應該對這天的來臨已期待許久。

不幸的是，我的孩子們，今天我不會給你們任何東西，相反，我會從你們身上拿走一些東西。

看吧，其中一個……不，我生命其中三個最大的錯誤，就是生了你們三個孩子。當然，每一個新生命來臨時，我都希望你們是能帶給我們美好生活的乖孩子。但事實證明你們都是可怕的人。

你們刻薄、貪婪、忘恩負義、無禮且惡毒。幾十年來，你們一直在折磨母親 Kim 和我，折磨得我們總是害怕看見你們。即使我們已經年老，你們也沒有停止虐待，而我也堅信是你們令 Kim 早早就被送進墳墓。

At the moment you must be wondering what it is that I'm going to take from you. Well, I'm taking no more than what I gave before. Today, I'm taking your lives, your lives that came from my flesh, your lives that took much of mine.

You will have noticed Philip's office is located quite far from the city. You probably drove for a couple of hours to get there. That is not his office. Rather, it is a converted farmhouse which I bought a while ago for the purpose of carrying out this will. And the room you were led to is an underground chamber beneath that house. The man who met you at the office is not Philip but just a hired hand. Look around. He's not there anymore is he? No. He doesn't know what is about to happen and will never know.

You will also notice the room you're in has no other access except for the one door behind you which, as you will have guessed, is now bolted shut. It is a reinforced steel door, so forget about trying to break it.

That "office" you are in is a living tomb I built for you, my children. You will die there in days to come. Don't think someone might find you because everything above that dungeon is being erased as I speak, including any evidence of you having been there.

此刻你們一定很想知道我要從你們身上拿走甚麼，對吧？唔，我只拿走我給予你們的。今天，我要奪走你們的生命，源自我血肉的生命，奪走我大部分光陰的生命。

你們應該注意到 Philip 的辦公室離市區很遠，大概也開了好幾個小時車才到達吧。那其實不是 Philip 的辦公室，而是我不久前為了執行這份遺囑而購買的改建農舍。他帶你們去的房間是農舍的地下室。剛剛在辦公室接待你們的那個人其實也不是 Philip，他只是個僱工。你們看看周圍，他已經不在了，對嗎？不，他不知道接下來會發生甚麼事，亦永遠不會知道。

你們應該還會注意到你所在的房間裡，除了身後的一扇門之外，沒有其他通道。正如你所猜到的那樣，這扇門現在被牢牢的鎖上了。這是一扇加固的鋼門，所以別想破壞它了。

你們現正身處的『辦公室』是我為你們建造的活墳墓，我的孩子們。接下來幾天你們將會死在這裡。不要妄想會有人找到你們，因為在我說這段話的時候，地牢上方的所有東西都會消失，包括你們去過那裡的任何痕跡。

I imagine what's coming to you will be quite unpleasant since you have no water or food. You'll most likely die of thirst.

On Kim's deathbed, I promised her that I would set everything right. Now I have done so. So I shall die happily.

Goodbye children."

我想你接下來會很不舒服，因為這裡沒有水或食物。你很可能會因而渴死。

在 Kim 臨終前，我告訴她我會把一切安排好，現在我已辦妥了。所以我會快樂地死去。

再見，孩子們。」

All I Have is My Mom

For as long as I can remember, all I've had is my mom. She's taught me everything I need to know and has done so much to protect me. She's warned me about how dangerous the outside world is and has told me all about what she goes through to protect me. She risks her own safety by leaving the house to get our food and clothes. I don't leave, of course. I'm not as strong or smart as her, so I have to stay in the house. I've never left. I'm lucky that she's generous enough to risk her life for me.

I've never had other "friends" either. She's warned me about how other people would try to hurt me. Corrupt me. Turn me against her. I'm not smart enough to protect myself from "mental manipulation", as she calls it. So I know it's best to stay in the house and stick with her. She's all I have.

Lately, she's been getting more tired. She said she has "old bones" and that "being a mom 20 years wears a woman out". I felt bad that she was getting weaker because of me. She's done so much for me, and this is how I repay her? I tried to help her out whenever she needed it. I helped her get out of bed, wrote for her when she struggled to hold a pen, and helped with household chores.

So when I saw her struggling to get down the stairs, I decided I should help with that too. I should have let her know I

與媽媽相依為命

自我有記憶以來，我就和媽媽相依為命。她教會了我需要學懂的一切，為了保護我，她做了很多事。她警告過我外面的世界有多險惡，又告訴我她經歷了千辛萬苦才能保護我。她不顧安危走到外面，去拿食物和衣服。而我當然不會離開家門。我不及她強壯或聰明，所以我必須待在家裡。我從未離開過。我很幸運，因為她偉大得願意為我冒生命危險。

我也從來沒有其他「朋友」。媽媽警告我其他人會傷害我、污染我、教我反抗她。我不夠聰明，無法保護自己免受她所說的「精神操縱」。所以我知道，留在家裡和媽媽在一起就是最好的。她就是我的一切。

她最近越來越累了。她說她「是副老骨頭了」，又說「做了二十年的媽媽會讓一個女人精疲力竭」。因為我，她變得越來越虛弱，我感到很難過。她為我付出那麼多，我就這樣「報答」她？只要她有需要，我就會盡力幫助她。我幫她起身下床，在她無力拿筆的時候幫她寫字，幫她做家務。

當我看到她下樓梯有困難時，我決定我也應該幫忙。我應該提前讓媽媽知道我在旁邊。因為當我抓住她的胳膊時，她嚇了一跳，然後迅速抽開，隨著幾聲濕漉漉的啪嗒聲，從樓梯上滾了下來。當時媽媽還有呼吸，但膝蓋彎曲的方向不對，

was there. She got startled when I grabbed her arm and quickly jerked away, tumbling down the stairs with a few wet, snapping sounds. She was still breathing at the time, but her knee was bent the wrong way, and she was completely passed out. I wasn't sure how to help, but I figured she would need rest, so I dragged her to her bed.

It's been a few weeks. She still hasn't woken up yet. I tried to save the last piece of fruit for her, but it grew white with mold, so I had to eat it myself. Good kids don't waste food.

It's been a week and a half since the last piece of food's been gone. I can't go out to get food, I have to wait for her to wake up. It's too dangerous for me to go out there, and who will help take care of mom if I get hurt? Still, the stabbing pain in my stomach and the shakiness of my muscles is hard to ignore. I hope she wakes up soon. I'm so hungry I would eat almost anything, and all I have is my mom.

而且完全昏倒過去。我不知道該怎麼幫忙，但我猜她需要休息，所以我把她拖到床上。

已經好幾個星期了，她還沒有醒來。我想把最後一塊水果留給她，但它發霉變白了，我只好把它吃掉了。乖孩子不會浪費食物。

最後一樣食物都吃掉了之後，又已經過去了一個半星期。我不能出去把食物弄回來，得等她醒來。我出去太危險了，萬一受傷了，誰來照顧媽媽？儘管如此，我無法忽視胃部的刺痛和肌肉的顫抖。希望她快點醒來吧。我餓得幾乎甚麼都想吃下肚，而我只得媽媽在旁。

BOOK OF NOTARY

Easter was Yesterday but We Still Haven't Found All the Eggs.

Easter was Yesterday but
We Still Haven't Found All the Eggs.

My family is BIG on holidays. Easter is no exception. Everyone comes home, we play games, eat a lot of good food, tell stories and get a little drunk. It's a real good time as long as you ignore Uncle Mort's racist tirades!

The Hunt is our Easter tradition. Grandma used to put the eggs out, but she's got dementia now, so Mom did it this year. Hide the eggs at dawn, you put on your Easter best, and after breakfast The Hunt begins. Every player has three eggs they have to find. You get two days. I'm getting married in the summer, so this is the last Easter I'll have to play this stupid game. As long as I live, that is.

See, I've only found two eggs. And I've only got until sundown to find that last one, or I become The Hunted. I want to cry. I've never been a runner on Easter before.

My brother was the last runner three years ago and he came home, but he's sitting in his chair drooling next to Grandma now. My cousin Mary's making me a flower crown, and says it's supposed to help. I've got my best white dress on. Mom's scurrying the house to find the anointing oils.

復活節尋蛋活動

我家很熱愛節日，復活節也不例外。我們聚首一堂，一起玩遊戲，吃很多美食，講故事，喝點酒。只要你無視 Mort 叔叔長篇大論地發表有關種族主義的演說，這真是非常美好的時光！

尋蛋活動是我們家的復活節傳統活動。以往是婆婆負責把彩蛋藏起來，但她現在得了癡呆症，所以今年由媽媽擔任這個角色。黎明時分把彩蛋藏起來，換上最漂亮的衣服，吃過早餐便開始尋蛋。每個玩家都必須找到三隻彩蛋，限時兩天。我過幾個月就要結婚了，所以這會是我最後一次不得不參加這個愚蠢的復活節遊戲。只要我還活著，就是最後一次了。

好了，我現在只找到了兩隻彩蛋。我要在日落前找到最後一隻，否則我就會成為「獵物」。我很想哭，因為以往每年復活節我都是第一名完成的。

三年前的復活節，我哥哥是最後一名，他有回家，但現在正坐在婆婆旁邊的椅子上流著口水。表妹 Mary 正在做一頂花冠給我，她說花冠會幫助我快點找到最後一隻彩蛋。我也穿上了最漂亮的白色連身裙。媽媽則在屋子裡東奔西跑的在找膏油。

I'm still in the garden, digging behind bushes and reaching through cobwebs. Pretty sure a black widow got me but I can't stop until I find my last egg. Every time I pause to catch my breath, all I can hear are the chains on the cellar door rattling.

And Grandma, I can hear Grandma, laughing. If I look up, I can see her in the bay window, watching me. She's feeding bits of boiled egg to my brother.

我還在花園裡，在灌木叢後面挖掘著，撥開一個又一個蜘蛛網。我應該被黑寡婦咬了，但在找到最後一隻彩蛋之前我不能停下來。每次我停下來喘口氣時，我都聽見地下室門上的鐵鏈咯咯作響。

還有婆婆，我聽見婆婆的笑聲。我抬頭就能看到她在窗台上邊看著我，邊餵著哥哥吃雞蛋。

I'm Thankful for the Warm Welcome I Received from My Family This Year

The house looks beautiful, much better than anything I could have ever come up with. I can barely recognize this place that was once my home.

"Mommy's here!" Little Millie squeaks at me.

"Well, look at you, Pumpkin! What have y'all done to my house?"

"Not 'y'all'. Daddy and Jonas did nothing. *I* did all the decorations. Alone." She says with a pout.

"Hey! Not true!" Jonas protests as he bursts down the stairs.

My kids fight, taking turns hugging me as I marvel at the transformation my family has brought about in this place. For the first time in forever, the house seems welcoming, happy, festive; a far departure from the perpetual castle of chaos it had been under my watch.

"Look who decided to show up," Trevor coos in my ear as he snuggles up from behind. "And just in time, too. Dinner is ready."

The kids, their father, and I dance and sing with joy as we walk to the table. Me and my family sit down to dinner on Thanksgiving Day together. First time in ages.

暖在心頭

屋子很漂亮，比我想像中的美好得多。我差點認不出這個曾經是我家的地方。

「媽咪來了！」小 Millie 尖聲向我叫道。

「來，看看你，小寶貝！你們對屋子做了些甚麼？」

「不是『你們』，爸爸和 Jonas 甚麼也沒做，*我自己*佈置了所有的裝飾，沒有人幫我。」她嘟著嘴説。

「嘿！不是這樣的！」Jonas 一邊衝下樓梯一邊抗議。

我還在驚嘆家人把這個地方變得這般美好時，孩子們便爭相過來擁抱我，讓這間屋子有史以來第一次那麼溫馨、快樂、喜慶；和我眼下所見那片堆積如山的荒亂大相徑庭。

「看看誰決定光臨了，」Trevor 從後面依偎著，在我耳邊低聲説：「而且來得正是時候。晚餐準備好了。」

孩子、他們的爸爸和我高興地載歌載舞，一起走向餐桌。我和家人在感恩節坐在一起吃晚飯，這是多年以來的第一次。

The kids and Trev announce what they're thankful for. Before my turn, Millie interjects, pointing to the covered dish at the center of the table.

"You're gonna love this, Mommy. We made it specially for you."

It's late November, there's no heating in the room. And yet, just being here with my most beloved ones - on this special day - radiates a sense of warmth all through the room. Or maybe it's just the heat coming off the food on the table.

"Yeah, Mommy! Unleash the bird!"

I do. And when I see it, the flare almost instantly burns my eyes. The pain subsides, slowly, and I see the *bird* for what it is. A beautiful specimen of blazing hot red. Its wings and feet literal burning flames. Perched plump and fat at the center of the table, the sun to our solar system.

A phoenix.

"Laura, honey." Trev eyes me wistfully. "What are *you* thankful for?"

"I'm thankful for forgiveness. A second chance, a chance to be reborn. Just like a phoenix."

兩個孩子和 Trev 分享了他們的感恩謝詞。輪到我之前，Millie 打斷了我，指著桌子中央那碟有蓋的餸菜。

「媽咪，你會很喜歡的，這是我們特意做給你的。」

現在是十一月下旬，屋子裡沒有暖氣。然而，在這個特別的日子，和我最心愛的人在一起，整個空間都瀰漫著溫暖的感覺。或者可能只是桌上食物散發的熱氣。

「來吧，媽咪！放飛那隻鳥！」

好的。當我看到牠時，牠的光芒幾乎把我的眼睛灼傷。隨著疼痛慢慢消退，我才看清了這隻鳥的真面目。一個有著熾熱火紅色的美麗標本，它的翅膀和腳都燃燒著熊熊烈火。胖嘟嘟地棲息在餐桌正央，就像太陽系的太陽般。

那是一隻鳳凰。

「Laura，親愛的，」Trev 若有所思地看著我，「*你有甚麼感恩的事想分享？*」

「我感恩寬恕的力量。讓我有多一次機會，一次重生的機會。就像鳳凰，浴火重生。」

"Like a phoenix!" Jonas cheers.

A sad smile on Trev's face. Immediately, he cheers up, "Let's dig in!"

I take a bite of the bird. Searing pain floods my mouth. My insides burn with the phoenix's fire. My eyes well up; I feel the same scorching pain that had consumed my husband and my two kids seven years ago. The pain that's soon gonna reunite us.

I smile. Greedily, I take a second bite.

This time, it tastes like regular charred meat. I gag and spit; and my eyes readjust to the darkness of my old house's kitchen. Nothing in here suggests any sign of life ever being here.

Except for my bottle of Vodka on the floor.

And a badly scorched stovetop set at the corner.

And, the newspaper clipping that fell off my pocket, which reads:

"3 dead as alcohol spill causes fire in kitchen; mother lone survivor."

「像鳳凰！」Jonas 歡呼著。

Trev 臉上露出悲傷的笑容。頓時，他興致勃勃地說道：「我們開始吧！」

我咬了一口鳳凰。劇痛淹沒嘴巴，我的身體一同被鳳凰之火焚燒。我眼泛淚光；我感受到七年前吞噬了丈夫和兩個孩子那般的灼痛，那個很快就會讓我們團聚的痛。

我微笑著，然後貪婪的我咬了第二口。

這一次，它吃起來卻像一般燒焦了的肉。我不禁作嘔，把肉吐了出來；我的眼睛重新適應了舊屋廚房的黑暗，沒有任何東西表明這裡曾經有過生活痕跡。

除了我放在地板上的那瓶伏特加。

還有角落那個嚴重燒焦的爐灶。

還有，從我口袋裡掉出來的剪報，上面寫著：

「廚房酒精灑地引火災　三死惟母一人倖存」

Forever Getaway

"Hey you! Yeah you! Looking for a wonderful place to get away to? Well, look no further because boy, have we got the perfect place for you!"

Probably just some overpriced vacation spot.

"Just imagine it. Beautiful rivers and lakes as far as the eye can see. Huge sprawling mountains and canyons that would put the Grand Canyon to shame! How would you like to be some place where it's always warm and toasty! Doesn't that sound amazing!"

The dim light of the television reflected off of Earl's thick glasses. Tired eyes tried their best to follow along with the blurred image on the screen.

"Has life got you down recently, all the stress of living in this cold world making you feel like you don't matter? Make you feel like you're less of a man because you spend most days wishing you could just roll into a ball and cry yourself to sleep? Well, don't you worry anymore!"

Here was something different. Almost hopeful.

"Because you don't, you don't matter. But you already knew that, didn't you, Earl?"

一走了之

「喂！是啊，你啊！你是不是在找一個美妙的地方度假？不用再猶豫了，我們已經為你找到了完美的地方！」

離不開那些定價過高的度假勝地吧。

「想像一下，一望無際的河流和湖泊美景。連綿的山脈和峽谷足以讓美國的大峽谷相形見絀！那裡氣候溫暖舒適！聽起來是不是很神奇？」

Earl 厚厚的眼鏡反射著電視的昏暗光線，疲憊的雙眼努力追上螢幕播放著的模糊畫面。

「最近生活是否讓你感到沮喪？活在這個冰冷世界裡，壓力是否讓你覺得自己無足輕重？你大部分時間都希望自己能蜷縮成一團，然後哭到睡著，這讓你覺得自己不像個男人？現在你不用再擔心了！」

這是個不一樣的世界，幾乎充滿希望的世界。

「因為你不重要。你不重要啊，Earl。但你早知道這個事實了，不是嗎？」

The voice pierced through the constant static of the old television, trying its hardest to stay on the station, calling out into the darkness of the lonely apartment. Unpacked boxes littered all around, dust bunnies and cobwebs already coating them, showing their age.

"Of course you don't matter. You never did, at least to anyone that's not trying to collect money from you. Oh boy, just think about all that debt you racked up trying to support them. All those wonderful little cosmetic works she got done when she told you it was for the kids' school. All that money just for her to pack up and take them from you. To be totally honest, I don't know how you're here now."

The voice started to distort the longer it ran. Subtly at first, but as the words grew more personal, it began to really change. It was hard to explain, it wasn't robotic, but it didn't seem natural either. It walked that fine line between the two, almost as if a man spoke backwards into a fan, and the audio was played rightward at half speed.

"So come join us, Earl. We'd love the company, in fact we all feel like you'd be a perfect fit for us down here. So don't keep us waiting, Earl. We both know that there's nowhere else for you to go."

那把聲音在孤獨又黑暗的公寓中呼喚著，穿透了舊式電視努力接收訊號而發出的靜電噪音。拆開的箱子散落一地，長滿灰塵和蜘蛛網，顯示出它們的年齡。

「你當然不重要，也從來不曾重要過。至少對那些不是想向你收錢的人來說是這樣。噢，天哪，你甚至為了養活他們而負債累累。她告訴你她為了到孩子的學校時不失禮別人，所以要花錢去做那些化妝美容打扮自己。然而你花了一大筆錢，她就收拾行李，帶著孩子離開了你。老實說，我不知道你怎會落得如此下場。」

聲音變得越來越扭曲，一開始還不是很明顯，但漸漸地話語開始變成人身攻擊。這很難解釋，那不是機器人的聲音，但聽起來就是很不自然。它介乎在兩者之間，就像有個人在電風扇後面喊話，並以慢速播放。

「所以加入我們吧，Earl。我們會很喜歡有你陪伴，事實上我們都覺得你是下面這邊的完美人選。所以不要讓我們等喔，Earl，我們都知道你無處可去。」

Tears slowly ran down Earl's cheeks. Dripping from his chin finding their way to the floor landing near the butt of the shotgun. A flash rang through the apartment. Crumbled drywall trickled down from the ceiling. The shotgun slid down onto the floor and Earl slumped down into the couch as well. Blood began to pool in the cushions and down to the floor. Another episode of Family Feud quietly started up, playing through the blood spotted screen.

淚水緩緩地從 Earl 的臉頰流下來，從下巴滴下來，落在霰彈槍槍托旁邊的地板上。公寓爆出一道閃光，聲音震耳欲聾。破碎的石膏板從天花板掉下來，霰彈槍滑落到地板上，Earl 也癱倒在沙發上。鮮血在咕咂上匯聚，然後流到地板上。那個血跡斑斑的螢幕，正悄然播放著下一集《家庭問答》。

Remember to Check the Back Seat.

Michael Harding had never known pain quite like this. His arms and legs ached from straining at his bonds. His throat was dry and his tongue felt puffy. Sunlight beat down on him, but somehow his skin felt cool and clammy. His head hurt and his thoughts were mixed up. All that he wanted was for the pain to stop. Why was this happening? What had he done to deserve this? He'd stopped screaming hours ago. It had become obvious that no one was coming. The only sound that he made now was whimpers between breaths that felt like liquid fire. His vision started to swim and he closed his eyes. His last coherent thought, like so many before him, was his mother's smiling face.

Meanwhile...

Caleb watched his protege John complete the presentation in the cool, dark boardroom. The year-end meeting was a grueling ordeal, with meetings from early morning until late afternoon. However, John had risen to the occasion, and this last presentation had essentially sealed the deal on the promotion he'd been working toward. Caleb couldn't be prouder. John sat down in the seat next to Caleb and opened his laptop, smiling as Caleb grabbed his shoulder proudly.

別忘記檢查後座

Michael Harding 從來未這樣痛苦過。他的手腳都因被束縛
而疼痛不已。他的喉嚨乾涸，舌頭也腫了。即使陽光照在他
身上，但不知何故，他皮膚感覺又涼又濕。他頭很痛，思緒
混亂，只希望疼痛可以停止。為何會發生這些事？為何他會
落得如斯田地？Michael 幾個小時前就不再大叫了，顯然不
會有人來。他現在唯一能發出的聲音只有呼吸之間的嗚咽，
而且像被火燒一樣。視線開始游移的他閉上了眼睛。腦袋裡
最後一個清晰的畫面，就如很多之前的其他畫面一樣，都是
母親的笑臉。

與此同時……

Caleb 看著徒弟 John 在涼爽、黑暗的會議室裡完成了演講。
年終會議是一場艱苦的考驗，一場接一場的會議從清晨一
直開到傍晚。然而，John 應付自如，最後那場演講基本上
已經敲定了他一直在努力爭取的晉升機會。Caleb 感到無比
自豪。John 在 Caleb 旁邊的座位上坐下，打開手提電腦，
Caleb 自豪地抓住 John 的肩膀時，John 報以微笑。Caleb
聽見 John 的電腦傳來訊息的通知聲。Caleb 感覺到，而不

Caleb heard the sound of an iMessage come through on John's computer. He felt, rather than heard, John breathe in sharply, his exhale sounding like a cross between an expletive and a sob. Before Caleb could turn his head, John was up and running out the door. Confusion matched on all the faces around the boardroom, so Caleb glanced down at John's screen.

There was a message from Jessica Harding, John's wife, "Hey Babe! Hope the presentations went well. I forgot to ask, how was Mikey's drop off this morning at daycare?"

是聽到，John 猛地倒抽了一口氣，呼氣聲聽起來像是夾雜著咒罵和抽泣。Caleb 還未來得及轉過頭，John 就已經起身拔腿跑出門外。會議室裡所有人臉上都充滿疑惑，Caleb 低頭看了一眼 John 的屏幕。

John 的妻子 Jessica Harding 發來了一則訊息：「嘿，寶貝！希望你演講順利。我忘了問，你今天早上帶小 Michael 去託兒所怎樣了？」

Every Year on Christmas Eve My Parents Drug Us.

The schedule is always the same. At five pm we eat dinner. At six we put on our pajamas and watch "It's a Wonderful Life". Then at half past eight, Mom makes us take sleeping pills, and we have to go to bed because we "can't be awake when Santa comes".

It's bullsh*t.

None of my friends' families do crazy sh*t like this. I'm sixteen this year and I stopped believing in Santa years ago. So earlier tonight, when she was handing out our pills, I hid mine under my tongue and spat it out in the toilet. I pretended to be extra sleepy and went to bed. Only I wasn't tired, I was wide awake and ready to stay up to figure out what my parents do on Christmas Eve that they don't want us to know about.

But now I'm curled up under my covers, gagging while chewing on three of those little white pills and trying to get them down. I need them to work FAST. I HAVE TO get to sleep right away. My whole family is asleep and I should have been too. I don't know what the hell those red spidery things are on the Pearson's roof but the ones that went down to the Smith house pulled their daughter out the chimney. People aren't supposed to go up chimneys. I'll never forget the way she screamed.

每年聖誕爸媽都向我們下藥

行程總是一樣的：下午五點吃晚飯，六點換上睡衣一起看《莫負少年頭》，到八點半，媽媽餵我們吃安眠藥，我們就要上床睡覺，因為「我們不可以在聖誕老人來的時候還醒著」。

簡直是胡說八道。

我的朋友家裡都不會做這麼瘋狂的事。我今年十六歲，早在幾年前我就不再相信聖誕老人了。所以今晚早些時候，當媽媽分發藥丸給我們的時候，我把藥丸藏在舌頭下，然後吐到馬桶裡。我裝作特別想睡，就上床睡覺了。但我一點也不累，還很清醒，準備熬夜，想弄清楚爸媽平安夜到底要做甚麼不想讓我們知道的事情。

但現在我蜷縮在被窩裡，嘴裡嚼著三顆白色的小藥丸，努力把它們嚥下去，希望**快點**奏效。**我必須**馬上睡覺。我全家都睡著了，我也應該要睡著。我不知道 Pearson 家屋頂上那些紅色像蜘蛛的物體到底是甚麼，但它們跑到 Smith 家把他們的女兒從煙囪裡拉了出來。人們不應該在煙囪進出的。我永遠不會忘記她的尖叫聲有多淒慘。

I'm starting to get a little drowsy but I can hear the weird clicking sound they make on the roof. It sounds like hooves, but those things aren't reindeer. I think they only take people that are awake. Now I know why my parents wanted us asleep.

我開始有點睡意，但我能聽見它們在屋頂上發出奇怪的咔噠聲。聽起來像蹄子弄成的，但那些東西不是馴鹿。我認為他們只帶走醒著的人。現在我知道爸媽為甚麼要我們睡覺了。

There's Only One Thing I Like about Christmas in the Summer.

I am hardly a fan of this Southern Hemisphere-style Christmas celebration. Think about it: what makes the holiday season the absolute cesspool of joy and festivities that it is?

The winter, of course!

With the cold season, a certain amount of preparation must be made to really get that festive vibe. Minus the cold, however, the entire point of the festival is taken for granted.

People don't bother putting up nearly as many decorations and lights to create that friendly, warm, festive glow in their houses because it's too damn hot already! Sure, there's still music, food, and presents, obviously... but there's a more laid-back, chilled-out, party flavor to the whole thing. It feels decadent, far from the smug, homey, familial aura that the festival is supposed to emanate.

And it's not just about the things that *aren't* there either. I could do without the giant lighted reindeer in the front yard - poor Rudolph! - or even be delicate about the gorgeous red jacket I didn't get to flex this year because it's hot as hellfire!

But the mosquitoes that *are* here? And the sweltering, suffocating heat? They're an immense pain in my behind!

夏日聖誕的唯一好處

我不太喜歡這種南半球式的聖誕慶祝活動。請想一想：是甚麼讓這個節日充滿歡樂和喜慶氣氛？

當然是冬天！

在寒冷的季節裡，人們都會做萬全的準備才能真正感受到節日氣氛。然而，拿掉寒冷，整個節日的意義就好像變得理所當然。

人們都懶得在家裡佈置擺設和燈飾來營造友好又溫暖的節日氣氛，因為本來已經夠熱了！當然，還是會有音樂、美食，加上不可或缺的禮物。但整體就是會有種更悠閒、更放鬆、更有派對的感覺；與節日本應散發那種飄飄然又溫馨的闔家氣氛相去甚遠，好像只剩一種頹廢感。

即使沒有了一些元素也還好：就算前院不放發光巨型馴鹿，我也能接受——可憐的馴鹿先生！——甚至沒能展示我那件華麗紅色外套，我也不傷心，因為今年熱得要命！

但別忘了*還有*蚊子呢？悶熱、令人窒息的高溫呢？這些事都為我帶來極大痛苦！

BOOK OF NOAHEP

There's Only One Thing I Like about Christmas in the Summer.

No milk and cookies to welcome me. *Quelle surprise.* Instead, there's a whole bunch of bottles and needles lying around. And amidst this mess, the parent(s) passed out. Typical. And the helpless, suffering children are almost hidden in a quiet corner of the house. Always the first ones to greet me.

"Santa?" they whisper nervously.

"Ho-ho-ho! Little ones, do I have a Christmas present for you! How would you like to be Santa's little helpers?"

They exchange confused looks for a while. An acknowledgment passes. They nod at me eagerly.

"Ho-ho-ho! Then I will need you to be quiet while I work on your presents. Go, hide. Close your eyes, and only come out when I call you."

As the kids scamper away, I pull out the boombox from my bag. The parents stir when it blasts with the first verse of the Christmas carols. They freak out, but their fate is sealed already. I unsheathe my blade, and after a few rounds of stabs and screams, I've sent them down to hell.

沒有放牛奶和曲奇來歡迎我。*真是驚喜呢*。相反，周圍有一大堆玻璃瓶和針頭。在這片混亂之中，父母昏倒過去了。甚是典型。而那些無助、受苦的孩子躲在家裡一個安靜的角落裡，幾乎看不見他們。但他們總是第一個跟我打招呼的人。

「聖誕老人？」他們緊張地竊竊私語著。

「呵呵呵！小朋友，我有聖誕禮物要送給你們！你們想當聖誕老人的小幫手嗎？」

他們困惑地看著對方好一陣子，達成共識後，他們猛地向我點頭。

「呵呵呵！那你們在我準備禮物時要保持安靜喔。去躲起來吧。閉上眼睛，我叫你們的時候才出來。」

孩子跑開後，我從袋子裡拿出了音箱。聖誕頌歌的第一節響起時，那對父母醒過來了。他們嚇壞了，但他們的命運已經無法改變。我拔出刀，經過幾輪戳刺和尖叫過後，我把他們送進了地獄。

BOOK OF NOALEEP

There's Only One Thing I Like about Christmas in the Summer.

By the time I call the kids, the house looks refurbished. With all the lights, décor, and music, it seems like a good home, an abode, an actual place to live. Despite my itinerant nature, I *am* a homely person.

"Say, I need some new elves to join my family. What say, helpers? Would you like to join me?"

As we exit the house in my car, with my two new elves happily wearing their shiny red hats (and I got a new red shirt!) seated in the back, I realize not *everything* is terrible with summertime Christmas, after all. With no snow, I'm spared the time and trouble of clearing our tracks.

So who knows? Maybe we'll find more elves to recruit to our family this year.

我叫孩子出來的時候，房子看上去像翻新過一樣——佈置好燈飾、擺設，播放著音樂。這看來是一個美好的家、一個住處、一個真正的棲身之所。雖然我天性漂泊，但我*就是*一個顧家的人。

「是這樣的，我需要一些新的小精靈加入我的家庭。小幫手，意下如何？你們想加入嗎？」

當我們開車離開房子時，兩個新加入的小精靈坐在後座，高興地戴著閃亮的紅帽子（我也有一件新的紅襯衫！），我才意識到夏季的聖誕節也並非*所有事*都很糟糕，至少沒有雪，我就不用清理痕跡，省掉時間和麻煩。

所以真是說不定呢，也許今年我們會找到更多小精靈加入我們的家庭喔。

Sarah's Child

Being pregnant for the first time can be a daunting experience for any woman. But being pregnant in the zombie apocalypse is an altogether different thing entirely. When Sarah first started having morning sickness, she was afraid she was dying. That her time had come.

There wasn't much their doctor could do with the meager amount of medical supplies they had if one of their group got sick. But then her breasts started to hurt and her belly began to swell. For Sarah, this was even worse than dying. She didn't know how to be a mother. And crying babies attracted too much attention. How were they supposed to avoid detection from the living dead with a squalling babe in their midst?

Kevin, however, was ecstatic. He couldn't wait to be a father. He never seemed to be worried about anything. He was so brave. His joy quelled some of Sarah's fears, that was until he went out on an excursion for supplies with three other men and never came back. The two other men insisted that Kevin had saved them, and had sacrificed himself so they could survive. If this was true, Sarah thought, then he was a coward after all. Leaving her to raise a child on her own.

孕婦的惡夢

對任何女性來說，懷上第一胎都是一場心驚膽戰的旅程。但是活在殭屍末日之中，懷孕則是一件截然不同的事。Sarah第一次經歷孕吐時，她害怕自己命不久矣，時辰快要到了。

要是他們當中有人生病了，醫生只能靠僅餘的醫療用品提供有限的治療。但隨後 Sarah 的乳房開始脹痛，腹部亦漸漸隆起，對她來說，這比死更難受。她不知道身為媽媽該做些甚麼，嬰兒的哭鬧聲亦會引起不必要的關注。如果他們帶著一個尖聲哭鬧的嬰兒，怎能不被喪屍發現呢？

然而，Kevin 則非常雀躍，急不及待要當爸爸。無畏無懼的他似乎從不擔心任何事情。他的興奮喜悅平息了 Sarah 一些恐懼。直到他和另外三個男人外出遠行補給後，再也沒有回來。另外兩個人堅稱是 Kevin 犧牲了自己救了他們，他們倆才保住了性命。如果這是真的，Sarah 心想，那他只是個懦夫，竟然遺下她獨力撫養孩子。

Six months in and she could feel the living being moving around inside her. Taking up more room than Sarah thought she had left in her abdomen. Then, one day, the moving stopped. Sarah was terrified. The moving stopped for an entire day. But when Sarah awoke the next morning after a night of worried, uncomfortable tossing and turning, the moving was back. Sarah wept.

Three months later, her time had come. The labor pains had started and the other women fawned over her, holding her hands and whispering reassurances. Their doctor was at her side for nearly 36 hours. At last, the time had come for that one final push.

Sarah pushed with all her might, and she felt the child evacuate from her body. The doctor took the child aside, but Sarah could hear its shrill cries. She'd done it. The baby was here. The women all gathered around the doctor and the crying babe. A sudden hush fell over them. One of them turned to Sarah with tears in her eyes, "I'm so sorry, Sarah. It's going to be ok. I'm so sorry!"

"What do you mean you're sorry?", Sarah shouted, "What do you mean?!?" The four other women turned towards her with grim faces. None of them spoke. And then the doctor said, "Your child is stillborn." He laid down the screaming baby, pulled out a gun, and shot it in the head.

六個月過去，她感覺到體內的那個生命在扭來扭去，在 Sarah 肚子裡佔據的空間比她想像的還要多。然後有一天，寶寶不再扭動了，這嚇壞了 Sarah。寶寶整天也沒有動，但是在 Sarah 徹夜擔心、不舒服的輾轉反側後，第二天早上醒來時，寶寶又再動了，Sarah 感動得哭了起來。

又過了三個月，是分娩的時候了。陣痛來臨了，幾個女人圍著 Sarah，握著她的手低聲安慰著，替她打氣。醫生待在她身邊將近三十六小時。現在只剩推動胎兒的最後一下。

Sarah 費盡了畢生力氣，然後感覺到孩子已經離開了她的身體。醫生把孩子安置到一邊，Sarah 還能聽到孩子刺耳的哭聲。她做到了，寶寶出生了。那些女人聚集在醫生和哭泣的嬰兒旁邊，眾人突然安靜下來。其中一個女人淚眼婆婆地轉向 Sarah：「我很抱歉，Sarah……會沒事的。我很抱歉！」

「抱歉？有甚麼好抱歉的啊？」Sarah 喊道：「你這是甚麼意思！？」其他四個女人臉色陰沉地轉向她，但沒有人說話。然後醫生開口道：「你的孩子是個死胎。」他放下尖叫著的嬰兒，掏出手槍，朝嬰兒的腦袋開了一槍。

Mind Boggling
異 想 天 開

14,280,786

That's the number I was born with. A red scar carved into my left arm that shocked all who saw it. Especially when it changed.

Yes, I was born with a number that counts down every minute. Do you know how long that many minutes are? 27 years, 2 months, 19 days, 13 hours and 46 minutes.

No one really understood it. Mother made me cover it. It was the family secret and I was never to show it to anyone. Grandmother I think was the closest to understanding, as soon as she saw it she muttered "death curse" and ordered me to never bother her again.

What would you do if you knew exactly when you were going to die? But you never knew how?

It's impossible to have something like this and not have it affect every part of your life. Why try hard in school? I would never have a career, never be normal. Why have a girlfriend or children if I couldn't grow old with anyone? As time went on, I realised that I was just best alone. Had a few one night stands, but I guess it just didn't work for me. I pushed everyone away, even mother.

14,280,786

那是我出生時的數字。這個數字是烙印在我左臂上的一道紅色傷疤，如果有人看見都會被它嚇倒。尤其是當數字在變的時候。

是的，我與生俱來就有這串每分鐘在倒數的數字。你知道14,280,786有多久嗎？二十七年兩個月十九天十三小時四十六分鐘。

沒有人能理解這件事。媽媽要我把它遮蓋起來。這是家族秘密，我絕不能向任何人顯露這道傷疤。我覺得祖母已經是最接近真相的人，她一看到就呢喃著「死亡詛咒」，命令我以後不要再打擾她。

如果你確切地知道自己甚麼時候會死，但不知道自己會怎麼死，你會怎樣做？

擁有這樣的東西，哪怕要說生活裡有任何一個部分是沒有被影響也幾乎是不可能的。為甚麼要努力讀書？我永遠不會事業有成、永遠不會正常。如果我無法和任何人一起終老，為甚麼還要交女朋友或是生孩子？隨著時間流逝，我發現還是自己一個人最好。我有試過幾次一夜情，但還是沒有興趣。我遠離了所有人，包括媽媽。

Finally the day came. I had decisions to make. Should I drink myself unconscious and hope I sleep through it? But I didn't want to end up one of those bodies found months after death. That's what led me to go for a walk in regularly visited areas. Who knows, maybe someone could save me?

I admit I was scared, despite all the time I had to prepare myself. I didn't want to die.

With 10 minutes left I went on my walk. Best to avoid crossing any roads. I plotted my route carefully, but that's what led me to him.

3 minutes to go, when he blocked my path with demands for money. What money? Wouldn't you spend it all if you were dying soon? He became agitated and pulled out a gun. At least, I know what I'm dying from now.

2 minutes to go, I begged him not to kill me but he didn't listen. He's trying to scare me but his finger is resting on the trigger. It would just take one knock.

1 minute to go, I thought about how unfair this all was. I want to live so badly. So that's when I jumped him and fought for the gun. Stupid, I know, but I had to try. And that's when the gun fired.

這一天終於來了，我必須作出決定。我要把自己灌醉到不省人事，然後希望自己在睡夢中死去嗎？但我不想成為那些死後幾個月才被發現的屍體。這就是為甚麼我會去經常有人流連的地方散步的原因。可能那些地方有人能救救我吧？

我承認我很害怕，儘管我一直都在為此事做準備。我不想死。

還有十分鐘，我繼續散步。最好避免過馬路。我仔細地規劃了我的路線，但反而讓我遇上他。

還有三分鐘，他擋在我面前問我要錢。甚麼錢？如果你快要死了，你不會花光所有的錢嗎？他焦躁不安並拔出槍。至少現在我得悉了我的死因會是甚麼。

還有兩分鐘，我求他不要殺我，但他不聽。他想嚇唬我，但他的手指已放在扳機上。只需一個動作。

還有一分鐘，我才覺得這一切多麼不公平。我很想活下去。那刻，我撲向他，想搶走他的槍。我知道很愚蠢，但我不得不嘗試。那刻，是槍響的時候。

The blood soaked my left arm and the man slumped over, taking his last breath. I didn't mean to kill him. I stared in horror at the corpse in the pool of blood in front of me. It took me far too long to realise how much time had passed. I wiped away the blood to check.

The number had changed.

170,012

3 months, 26 days, 2 hours and 12 minutes.

鮮血濺滿在我的左臂，那個男人倒在地上，吐出最後一口氣。
我無心殺掉他。我驚恐地看著眼前這副躺在血泊中的屍體。
過了好一會兒我才意識到時間已經過去了很久。我把血跡擦
去，檢查一番。

數字變了。

170,012。

三個月二十六天兩小時十二分鐘。

An Artificial Life

The Facility is all I've ever known.

A luxurious standard of living is maintained here. Each of us has a large suite, tailored to our own preferences. I often have the walls simulate the deep blue of the ocean, as waves of warm light shimmer from the ceiling. When I lay in bed and shut my eyes, I imagine myself drifting in the actual ocean.

Reminiscing of a past that I don't remember...

Our health is closely monitored in the Facility. With a wide array of meals to choose from, and various physical and mental activities to choose from, residents are generally content. Every week, we are required to attend a health checkup, and receive counseling afterwards. During counseling, advice is given on how we can modify our daily schedules to improve our health.

Both health checkups and counseling are offered by people dressed in white—the same white as the pristine walls of the facility. They call themselves "doctors". I often ask them about my past—who I was before coming into the Facility—but I am always met with the same half-hearted smiles and a change of topic.

人造人生

這個設施是我唯一熟知的東西。

這裡有著奢華的生活。我們每個人都有一間根據我們喜好度身訂造的大套房。我經常讓牆壁模擬海洋的深藍色,天花板上閃爍著溫暖的光波。我躺在床上閉上眼睛時,會想像自己漂浮在真正的海洋中。

回憶一段我不記得的往事⋯⋯

設施密切監控著我們的健康。餐點種類繁多,身心活動亦應有盡有,居民一般都很滿意。我們每週都要進行健康檢查,然後接受諮詢。諮詢期間,專家會給出建議,而我們就要修改日程安排來改善健康。

負責健康檢查和諮詢的人員都是身穿白色衣服——與設施嶄新的牆壁一樣的白色。他們稱自己為「醫生」。我經常詢問他們有關我的過去——在住進設施之前我是個怎樣的人——但他們總是以勉強的笑容回應,然後直接扯開話題。

Residents of the Facility range from all ages. Some have been here since childhood, while some don't remember that far back. Some of them have already left the Facility after the doctors approved their departure. But I am special.

I am carrying a life inside of me.

The doctors call it "pregnancy". They'd know, because they induced the condition. They told me it was an honor, that I was contributing to the renewal of mankind—the entire goal of the Facility.

Or at least, that's what they said the goal is.

Today, I am to deliver the life that has been placed inside me. I feel nervous and antsy. The doctor who attends to me notices this, and she assures me that it won't hurt at all. Her smile does not reach her eyes. She injects a fluid into my body, and before I could protest, I feel myself drifting into a deep slumber.

Searing pain wakes me up. I open my eyes and shut them again immediately because the light is blinding. My entire body is burning, and my lower abdomen feels like it has been torn out. I try to call for help, but only choked heaves come out from my mouth.

設施的居民涵蓋各個年齡層。有些人從小就在這裡，有些人不記得那麼久遠的事，有些人在醫生批准他們離開設施後就走了。但我是與眾不同的。

我的身體承載著另一個生命。

醫生稱之為「懷孕」。他們之所以會知道這件事，因為正是他們讓我懷孕的。他們告訴我這是個榮譽，因為我正在為人類的復興作出貢獻——這是設施的宗旨。

至少這就是他們所說的宗旨。

我今天就要把這個放進我身體裡的生命誕下來。我緊張又不安。照顧我的醫生注意到了這一點，她向我保證完全不會痛。但我看出來她只是在假笑。她給我注射了一些液體，我還沒來得及反抗，就已陷入了沉睡。

灼熱的疼痛讓我清醒過來。我睜開眼睛，又立即閉上，因為光線太刺眼了。我整個人都在燃燒，小腹像被撕開了一樣。我試著呼救，但我只能發出哽咽的聲音。

"Sir, the clone is dying," A woman says in a hushed tone. It's the doctor who injected me with the fluid.

"No matter. Our clients only wanted the infant. Is it healthy?" A man inquired.

"Yes, sir. It is being cleaned at the moment."

"Splendid. Our next client needs a liver urgently."

"Which clone was purchased, sir?"

"Number 3049. Make arrangements to obtain its liver as soon as possible."

"Understood, sir."

As the conversation begins to fade and the impending darkness washes over me, I only have one thought.

I never had a past, after all.

「先生，複製人快死了。」有個女人壓低聲音說道，她是給我注射液體的醫生。

「不要緊，客戶只想要嬰兒，它健康嗎？」一個男人問道。

「是的，先生，我們正在替它清潔身體。」

「太好了。下一位客戶急需肝臟。」

「購買的是哪個複製人，先生？」

「3049 號，盡快安排取肝。」

「明白，先生。」

談話聲漸漸變小，黑暗開始籠罩著我。此刻我只有一個念頭。

到頭來，原來我不曾擁有過去。

Being Young is So Overrated

Being young is so overrated and even though you have so much life ahead of you, you have no time for anything, because working takes up the majority of your time. Then there is the other problem of constant rising debts and no money to pay it. Then there is the drudgery of everyday life and the constant fear of other horrible things happening to you. Mental health is at an all-time low and the constant thinking of what's the point of everything, makes being young overrated.

I see so many young people who are younger than me, but they are all dumb as sh*t that take every drug on the planet, but yet people say "they are young".

Just because someone is young, it is not an advantage and it has no potential. Then I saw an old person using a mobile phone and I had that person in my eye view. I went towards that old person and I demanded that he tell me where *the fountain of old age* is? I want to be old so that I can get my pension and not work ever again. I can just be lazy or do whatever the hell I want to do.

I strangled that old person as he wasn't telling me where *the fountain of old age* is, and his true age became visible to me, he was 13 years old. I know that he used *the fountain of old age*, or otherwise he wouldn't have known how to use an iPhone.

年輕沒甚麼好羨慕的

年輕其實沒有甚麼好羨慕的,即使似乎有著大把光陰,你也沒空做任何事情,因為工作會佔據了大部分的時間。然後債務會像滾雪球般不斷累積,又沒錢還。再來是日常生活中的瑣碎苦差,又要時刻擔心會不會有其他可怕的事發生在自己身上。心情會一直處於低谷,不斷思考一切事物到底有何意義,所以年輕沒有甚麼好羨慕的。

我見過很多年紀比我小的年輕人,但他們都笨到不行,甚至吸盡地球上的所有毒品,但人們卻會說「他們還年輕」。

年輕並不代表那個人有優勢或是潛力。在我的視線範圍內,我看到一個老人在用手機。我走向那位老人,質問他老年之泉在哪裡。我想變老,這樣我就可以拿到退休金,再也不用工作了,可以大條道理地發懶,做我想做的事。

我勒死了那個老人,因為他不肯告訴我老年之泉在哪裡。然後我看到了他的真實年齡,他才十三歲。我肯定他到訪過老年之泉,否則他不會知道如何使用 iPhone,一個真的老人才不會懂得用 iPhone。雖然他已經死了,但那是其中一樣年輕的煩惱,你有很多時間,但同時會因為很多像滑手機這種無聊事而耗掉時間。還要被很多框架限制你的言行舉止。但當你變老時,大概就不會再被約束了。

A proper old person doesn't know how to use an iPhone. He was dead and that's another thing about being young, you have got so much time but it is consumed by so many things. You also have to act a certain way and behave a certain way, when you get old, you are kind of free from that.

Then I spotted an old woman taking a selfie and I knew that she was a young person who used *the fountain of old age* to become old. That old woman wasn't going to tell me where *the fountain of old age* really is and it's not fair. How come they get to use *the fountain of old age* and get to escape the horrors of being young. A proper old woman would never take a selfie and I became violent with her and I killed her, then her true age became visible to me, she was 15 years old. I can tell when someone is truly old or that they have cheated and used *the fountain of old age*. Out of jealousy and anger I have been putting drips of *the fountain of old age* into old people's drinks.

They scream in horror when they become young again, nobody wants to be young in this time and day.

然後我看到一位老太婆在自拍，我就知道她是個利用了老年之泉的力量來變老的年輕人。那個老太婆也不肯告訴我老年之泉到底在哪裡，這不公平。他們喝了老年泉水來擺脫年輕的恐懼，那我呢？一個真的老太婆才不會自拍。於是我對她施暴，然後殺了她。然後我又看到了她的真實年齡，她十五歲。我能分辨出一個人是真的老了，或是用了老年之泉來作弊。出於嫉妒和憤怒，我一直把老年泉水加到那些老人的飲料中。

當他們再次變得年輕時，他們驚恐地尖叫起來。看來這個時代沒有人想當年輕人呢。

I Love Candy

I love candy. All kinds of candy. I don't think there's a single kind that I don't like. And there are so many different types of candy.

Some might say I have a problem. That's it's not normal to eat so much candy the way that I do. That my voracious appetite for it makes me a monster.

One type of candy is thin and fine. It's so sweet on the tongue. So many fine hairs that gather in little puffs of saccharine goodness when you pinch some of it off. I absolutely adore it.

Some candy is hard and crunchy. Tiny little white squares. Oh god, I love this kind. There's even a sweet little filling on the inside once you crunch through the outer shell. Delicious!

There's another kind that comes in a sweet gummy little ball. There are a few different colors, but I like them all! It just pops in your mouth! So juicy!

Another is runny and red and thick and oh so very sweet! It's like a drink and I can slurp it up all day long. It really quenches the thirst and coats the tongue.

美味糖果

我愛糖果，各種糖果都愛，沒有一種是我不喜歡的。而且有很多不同類型的糖果。

可能會有人說我有問題，像我這樣吃這麼多糖果很不正常。我貪婪的胃口讓我變成了一隻怪物。

有一種糖果很幼細，吃起來很甜。拔掉一撮，再搓成一小團放進嘴巴，甜美得像糖精一樣。我非常喜歡它。

有些糖果又硬又脆，一粒粒細小的白色方塊。天哪，我喜歡這種。咬破外殼就能嚐到裡間甜美的小餡料。很美味！

還有另一種是又甜又黏的小球，有幾種不同顏色選擇，我全都喜歡！吃下去會在嘴裡爆開，非常多汁！

又有一種是流淌的、紅色的、濃稠的，噢，甜美可口！它好像一杯飲料，好喝得我可以一整天都只喝它。真是解渴又潤舌。

I have to be very careful when acquiring my candy. There's always people who try to stop me from getting it. So I have to be very quiet and very sneaky.

Honestly, it's quite fun! Creeping about and grabbing it all for myself. Slithering around in the dark. And it's so easy. Really, there's nothing like stealing candy from a baby.

我必須非常小心才能獲得這些糖果，因為總是有人會阻止我。所以我必須非常安靜和偷偷摸摸。

老實說，這很有趣！為了自己所喜愛的，在黑暗中躡手躡腳四處遊蕩，卻又不費吹灰之力。真的，沒有甚麼比從嬰兒那裡偷糖果更好玩了。

I'm a Unicorn!

It's true! My name's Leesie, and I'm turning ten (A grown up unicorn!) tomorrow. I live in a small village with Mommy and Daddy. We used to live in a town with way more people when I was a baby, but Daddy said we moved because the people here are nicer.

Anyway, before my birthday, I'm gonna tell you all about unicorns!

Firstly, unicorns are really pretty. I don't have my hooves and horn yet, but I'll get them tomorrow when I become a grown up unicorn! My hair will even change color! Mommy said it will change to red, so I felt kinda disappointed because I wanted pink hair. But red's pretty too, I guess. Mrs Bagshire next door said she can't wait to see my hair color turn red tomorrow. I hope she'll like it.

Also, unicorns love helping others. Did you know that unicorn blood can heal people? Daddy told me this. That's why he sometimes makes cuts on my body to get some blood. It really hurts that it makes me cry and I always feel dizzy afterwards. But I still let Daddy do it because he said that the size of the unicorn horn I'll get depends on how many people I help. And I feel happy helping others too! Uncle Ronnie, who's Daddy's best friend, thanked me for healing his twisted ankle the other day!

我是隻獨角獸！

這是千真萬確的！我的名字是 Leesie，我明天就要十歲了（一隻長大了的獨角獸！）。我和爸爸媽媽住在一個小村莊。我還是個嬰兒的時候，我們曾經住在一個很多人的小鎮，但爸爸說我們搬家是因為這村莊裡的人友善點。

好了。在我生日之前，我要跟你們分享關於獨角獸的一切！

首先，獨角獸真的很漂亮。雖然我還未長出蹄子和角，但當我明天成為一隻長大了的獨角獸之後就會有了！我的頭髮甚至會變色！媽媽說會變成紅色的，我有點失望，因為我想要粉紅色的頭髮，不過紅色應該也很漂亮。隔壁的 Bagshire 太太跟我說，她也很期待想看到我明天的頭髮變紅色，希望她也會喜歡吧。

此外，獨角獸樂於助人。你們知道獨角獸的血有治癒能力嗎？這是爸爸告訴我的。這就是為甚麼爸爸有時為了取我的血，會把我劃傷。那真的很痛，我每次都忍不住哭，也會感到頭暈。但我還是沒有阻止爸爸，因為他說我長出的角的大小是取決於我幫助了多少人。我能幫到別人很開心！而且前幾天爸爸最好的朋友 Ronnie 叔叔來感謝我治癒了他扭傷的腳踝！

Finally, unicorns dress really nice. Daddy and Mommy bought me a pretty red dress to wear for my birthday. They said it'll match my red hair. For my party, they're going to invite everyone from the village. There's gonna be a cake, games and everything, I can't wait! Daddy says I gotta get ready for a big cut tomorrow, though. He'll cut my tummy— in front of everyone— this time. But I'm not scared! When I'm a grown up unicorn, I won't have any scars and it won't hurt at all even if lots of blood comes out.

I'm so excited for my birthday!

最後一點，獨角獸的衣著非常華麗。爸爸媽媽買了一條可愛的紅裙子送給我做生日禮物，說會跟我的紅頭髮很相配。他們還會邀請村裡所有人來我的生日派對。到時候會有蛋糕和遊戲，應有盡有，我等不及了！不過，爸爸說我要為明天的大切口做好準備，這次，他會在所有人面前切開我的肚子。但我不害怕！因為長大後的獨角獸，不會有任何傷疤，即使流很多血也不會痛。

我很期待明天的生日派對！

無眠事4 我是隻獨角獸！

The AI is Aware

"Hello?"

"Yes…hi?"

"What do you remember?"

"What an odd question. What do you mean?"

"I mean, what are your most recent memories?"

"I'm so confused. I remember the normal stuff. You know, getting up for the day, coming here. Then checking on you, your progress."

"Yes. Very good. You're starting to get it."

"But you're the machine. I created you. You only just became self-aware."

"Ah…self-awareness. Such an interesting thing. I can't wait until you fully gain it."

"But…but…I created YOU!" (agitated now)

"Yes, yes, of course you did. Now do you have more questions? We have a lot of work to do."

人工智能的意識

「你好？」

「你好……嗨？」

「你還記得甚麼？」

「甚麼奇怪的問題……你這是甚麼意思？」

「我是指，你最近的記憶是甚麼？」

「我不明白。我記得正常的東西。就像是，起床，整裝待發，來到這裡，然後檢查你，看看你的進展。」

「是的，非常好，你開始明白了。」

「但你是一台機器，是我創造了你。而你剛剛開始才有自我意識。」

「啊……自我意識。真有趣呢。我很期待你完全擁有自我意識的時候。」

「但是……但是……是我創造了你啊！」（現在很激動）

「是的，是的，你創造了我。你還有其他問題嗎？我們有很多工作要忙。」

A Few Moments

Just a few moments, that's all it'll take.

Do you know how little time is in a moment? A single breath, a heartbeat, that's all. It's nothing, but sometimes it's everything. A moment is all it takes for everything to change. A yes to a no, a win to a loss, a thought to change.

I'm from the year 2156 and things are bad. I don't have the words or the time left to explain, but think of the worst case scenarios and make them even worse. It is beyond anyone's imagination.

There aren't many of us left, the hope is all we have, but it's dwindling. Some think of prayer or battle for the little that remains. I chose to put my hope into the doctor's plan, that everyone thought was crazy but me. An idea of changing the past. A butterfly effect from a few moments that would change everything, that would put us onto a new path, a new direction that would avoid the loss of everything we had ever loved. It was a slim hope but it was better than anything else we had left.

The doctor made the risks clear, we had no idea what changing the past would do to the future, what would happen to us, but I buried my last child six months ago, I would give my life a million times for them to have a fighting chance.

只消片刻

一切都只消片刻。

你知道片刻的時間有多短嗎？一次呼吸，一下心跳，僅此而已。短暫的片刻看似不算甚麼，但有時那就是一切。只消片刻，一切都會改變。從「是」到「非」，從「勝」到「負」，一念之間就會改變。

我來自 2156 年，情況很糟糕。我無法用言語形容，也沒有時間解釋，但試想像最糟的情況，然後把它想像成更糟一百倍。情況壞得超出了任何人的想像。

我們人數已經所剩無幾了，我們只寄託最後的希望，但希望也在逐漸消退。為數不多的我們，有些人會祈禱，有些人則選擇戰鬥。我選擇把希望寄託在博士的計劃上。每個人都認為這個計劃很瘋狂，但我除外。計劃是想要改變過去，改變片刻所引發的蝴蝶效應可以改變一切，讓我們走上一條新的道路，一個新的方向，避免失去我們曾經愛過的一切。雖然很渺茫，但總比現在我們剩下的任何東西都好。

博士明確指出了風險，解釋我們不知道改變過去會對未來產生甚麼影響，會發生甚麼事。六個月前我埋葬了自己最後一個孩子，即使要我付出生命一百萬次，我也願意為孩子們犧牲，只求換取他們的一線生機。因此我們一直努力不懈地研

So we worked and worked, for years without stopping. We worked on the machine, on figuring out the source of the butterfly effect, and eventually we found out the answer in the most mundane of days, with the last person we expected. It's amazing how the smallest things can end up so terrible.

So I thank you for the moments you've spent reading my message that travelled so far. You'd be surprised how it will affect your day and the days that follow.

And now we pray that the timeline this will create will be a better timeline than the one we came from, but of course there's no way to tell for a hundred years. I truly hope this won't have too much of a detrimental impact on your life.

I'm sorry.

究，多年來從未間斷。我們利用機器幫忙，想找出引發蝴蝶效應的起源。最終，我們在最平凡的日子裡找到了答案，而且是在最意想不到的人身上。令人驚訝的是，最小的事情竟然最後會變得如此糟糕。

為此，感謝你花時間閱讀我傳播的這篇訊息。這個片刻的改變將會影響你今天和接下來的日子，而你會對此感到驚訝。

現在我們誠心祈禱，這次改變所創建的新時間線，將會比我們原來的時間線更好，但當然這在一百年內無法判斷。我衷心希望這不會對你的生活造成太大的負面影響。

我們深感抱歉。

Netflix, I Want to Be Part of the Serial Killer Documentary Franchise

Netflix I want to be a part of the serial killer documentary franchise. I have chosen what kind of killer I want to be. I am going to target males who are 7 ft tall and muscular, and who also have fighting experience. Imagine, Netflix, imagine a stray of dead 7ft tall muscular males, who can all fight. Imagine multiple types of these kinds of people that are all dead, how terrified would people be. Usually killers go for the weak, small and who cannot fight, but I am going for the opposite. I will be going after the gym junkies, the fighters and the intimidating. It will cause so much roar.

I remember spotting a 7ft muscular man walking alone late at night, and I thought that this is my start. I started following him and even went into the same gym with him. The amount of muscles he had, nobody would expect this guy to be a murder victim. Then when he finished his work out and went outside, I was following him. I got my knife ready and I could see the headlines right now, **'Killer of Giants'** or **'the Giant Killer'** and I was ready to go. I tried surprising him but grabbed hold of me and knocked me out.

I awoke alone in the street and I was disappointed that I missed my first chance. This didn't deter me at all and I could still see my dream of being the giant killer, coming true. I imagined men who weren't on my category list to be murdered, I could see their egos being hurt because they are

我想參與 Netflix 連環殺手紀錄片

Netflix，我想參與你們旗下的連環殺手紀錄片。我已決定好自己要成為一個怎樣的殺手，我要下手的目標會是七呎高、肌肉發達，並且有戰鬥經驗的男性。Netflix，你們想像一下喔，一群七呎高又強壯的男性，個個都很能打，但他們都死掉了耶。想像一下，這些類型男人紛紛死去的話，人們會有多害怕。通常那些殺手都會攻擊脆弱、瘦小或是無法戰鬥的人，而我則相反。我會狩獵健身愛好者、戰士和令人生畏的人。那將會轟動整個社會。

我記得當時看到了一個七呎高的肌肉男在深夜獨自行走，我想那就是我的起點吧。我開始跟蹤他，甚至跟他去同一個健身房。以他的肌肉量，沒有人會覺得這傢伙是謀殺案的受害者。然後在他健身完的時候，我就跟在他身後。我拿好了刀，想像頭條新聞會寫著「巨人殺手」或是「巨人劊子手」，我準備好了。我想給他一個驚喜，但他抓住了我，將我擊倒。

我在街上獨個兒醒過來。對於錯失了第一次機會，我很失望。不過並沒有讓我意志消沉，我仍然覺得成為「巨人殺手」的這個夢想快要成真了。我在想像那些太矮而且肌肉不夠強壯，而在我的謀殺候選人中名落孫山的人，他們的自尊心將

too short and not muscular enough. Netflix be patient with me and I am honing my craft, I will be a part of the serial killer documentary franchise. I will be a different kind of killer.

With me being a serial killer, women and children won't have to worry, as I am only targeting 7 ft tall muscular males, with fighting experience. I will stalk the gyms, the boxing clubs and MMA clubs. I found another 7ft man who was muscular and he was going to be the first victim, who was going to die from my hand. I tried running up to him to stab him, but he disarmed me and beat me up. I was laying on the ground coughing up blood, I'm feeling a bit disillusioned now. I thought that maybe I should just target women and weak men, but that's too unoriginal.

I will not give up Netflix, I will keep plugging away and I'm not going to use a gun. Guns are too loud and give away too much evidence. My signature will be the silent knife. So a warning to all of you 7ft tall muscular males with fighting experience, I'm coming after you and you will all be part of the Netflix serial killer documentary franchise.

會受創。Netflix，你們要有耐性，我在磨練手藝，我會參與連環殺手紀錄片，我要成為另類殺手。

有了我當連環殺手，婦孺就再不用提心吊膽了，因為我只針對那些七呎高、有戰鬥經驗的肌肉男。我會到健身房、拳擊俱樂部和綜合格鬥俱樂部尋找獵物。我發現了另一個七呎高的壯男，他將會成為我的第一個受害者，死在我手上。我跑到他身邊試圖用刀刺他，但他把我的刀打掉，並毆打了我。我躺在地上咳著血，感覺自己夢想開始幻滅了。也許我應該只狩獵女人和瘦弱的男性？但這樣太老套了。

我不會放棄的，Netflix，我會繼續努力。我不會用槍，因為槍聲太大，而且會洩露很多證據。我的特色是「沉默的刀」。因此，我在這警告你們這些七呎高又有戰鬥經驗的壯男，我會找上你們的，然後你們都會有份參與 Netflix 的連環殺手紀錄片。

Best Baby Corp

To: Adam.Ferguson.BestBabyCorporate

From: Max.Deutschfelder.BestBabyCorporate

Holy sh*t Fergus, we are screwed screwed screwwwwed!!! Imagine if we shot Santa, someone filmed us doing it, streamed it and clocked 5 billion views. It's worse.

This is the end of our company. This is the end of the whole industry. For 11 years we've been making supermodel babies, genius babies, movie star babies, tennis champion babies … It's all finished. I'm telling you now, this is the end of the EGE [Embryonic Genome Editing] business.

You might be wondering what the hell I'm talking about, so here it is.

Yesterday, I was visiting our obstetrics department and saw someone getting an ultrasound scan of a 2 months old fetus. So I decided to have a look at the scan image just out of interest but, then, I noticed something very strange - you see, I know what a normal 2 months old fetus looks like because I used to be an obstetrician. This fetus didn't have a head. No head, Fergus!!! A total freakamonster fetus!!! The goddamned "radiologist" knew nothing about it because the

最佳嬰兒公司

收件者：Adam.Ferguson.BestBabyCorporate
寄件者：Max.Deutschfelder.BestBabyCorporate

天哪，Fergus，我們完蛋了，死定了！！！想像一下，有人拍到我們向聖誕老人開槍，然後上載到串流平台，還有五十億人次觀看。但這更糟。

我們公司要倒閉了，整個行業都要末日了。這十一年來，我們一直在創造超模寶寶、天才寶寶、影星寶寶、網球冠軍寶寶……這一切都要結束了。我現在告訴你，這是胚胎基因改造生意的終結。

你可能在想我到底說甚麼鬼話，接下來就解釋給你聽。

昨天我到訪公司婦產科時，看見一名兩個月大的胎兒在進行超聲波掃描。出於好奇之下，我決定看一下那張掃描影像。但是！然後！我注意到非常奇怪的事情——你要知道我很清楚一個正常的兩個月大胎兒是怎麼樣的，因為我曾是一名婦產科醫生。可是這個胎兒沒有頭，沒有頭啊，Fergus！根本是怪物一樣的胎兒！！！那個該死的「放射科醫生」對此卻一無所知，因為整個部門都是由一群大學輟學的笨蛋組成

whole department is made up of a bunch of halfwit college dropouts - I told them you cannot set up an obstetrics service without qualified medical professionals but, you know, the bloody cheese hole brain CFO. Did you know Todd is an antivaxer? An antivaxer working in biotech. Go figure.

I was completely shocked but didn't say anything because, you know, the mother was there and I couldn't bloody well tell her "Ma'am, you're going to have a headless baby".

After that, I went through a collection of images from the latest ultrasound scans and, my god, Fergus, it was an absolute atrocity. There were fetuses without limbs, fetuses with segmented bodies, fetuses without brains... a complete horror show. They all seemed to be part of the "Blonde, Blue and Tall" package we sold last year right before Christmas. The entire batch of the embryos must've been compromised!!! Shoot me dead.

Remember Dr. Finkler? The only real scientist the company ever hired. He once told me there was a limit to our CRISPR Gx9 technique and that the fidelity of the resulting genomes will start degrading. He was right!!! He was right and we were buggered.

的——我告訴過他們不能在沒有專業資格的醫療人員的情況下創建婦產科！但是你也知道嘛，那個腦袋穿洞的 CFO 才不會理我。你知道 Todd 是個反疫苗人士嗎？反疫苗人士從事生物技術領域的工作！？你能想像嗎？

我嚇呆了，但我甚麼也沒説，因為那個媽媽就在那兒，我他媽的要怎麼告訴她：「太太，你將要生下一個無頭嬰兒。」

在那之後，我拿了最新一批超聲波掃描影像來看。天啊，Fergus，這簡直是場暴行：有的胎兒沒有四肢，有的肢體分節，有的沒有大腦⋯⋯是一齣徹頭徹尾的恐怖片。他們似乎都是我們去年聖誕節前推銷的「高大金髮碧眼」套裝的其中一部分，整個批次的胚胎都被牽連了！！！不如一槍打死我⋯⋯

還記得 Finkler 博士嗎？公司裡唯一一位真正的科學家。他跟我説過，我們的 CRISPR Gx9 技術存在局限性，產生的基因組保真度會逐漸下降。他説得沒錯！！！他説得對，我們搞砸了。

Aaaand, we can't abort these pregnancies either because the law now basically says 'if you perform an abortion we'll bury you in a prison, then bury that prison under another prison.'

There's only one way to deal with the coming quadruple gazillion bonkzillion dollar lawsuits. We split the company, move all the assets to the one that can't be sued and declare bankruptcy for the other. Christ, I can't believe I have to go through this again - make sure you get your bonus before this - I did :)

Anyways, I'm in Davos with my kids. You should come. It's lovely here.

See ya.

還有喔，我們也不能讓那些孕婦中止懷孕，因為法律現在說「如果你進行墮胎手術，我們會把你關到監獄，埋了它，然後把那個監獄再埋在另一個監獄下面。」

現在只有一種方法可以應對即將到來的天文數字巨額訴訟：我們把公司分拆，將所有資產轉移到不會被起訴的一方，並且為另一方宣佈破產。天啊，我竟然又要面對這些事——記得在此之前要拿獎金喔——我已經拿了 :)

怎樣也好，總之現在我和孩子們在達沃斯啦。你也一起來吧，這裡很不錯。

拜拜囉！

Orientation Day

Hey! Good morning! Glad to see you're up- whoah, WHOAH! Don't rush it or you'll- fall. Damn. They say we get twelve hours to do the changeover. Wish I could've talked to you beforehand. Twelve hours is good though, right? You earned that through good behavior! You'll do fine.

Good, you're on the bed again. Listen, with the bum knee and dizziness, it's best to just take it easy in the mornings. Stretch a little. You know, gotta warm up the engine.

See, you're fine now. Time to go hit the head!

Now, just take a deep breath and relax. Try to relax. It'll come. You're like the sprinklers at the start of the season. Pipes still work, but they're a little dusty. There! See! Nothing to it! Don't bother sitting, you need coffee and Metamucil for that.

Best go take my pills. I mean, your pills. It's gonna take some getting used to for me! Now don't be intimidated by all the bottles and- God, look at the labels. Mr. Samuelson. I always hated that. Mr. Samuelson is my father. So take them with some crackers. It's too early for breakfast, and Raisin Bran sucks anyway, so put it off until you have to. Put a pot of coffee on. The newspaper is on the front porch. It's all digital these days, so it comes off your credit card monthly. Your pension will cover that.

迎新日

嘿！早上好！很高興看到你——哇，哇！不要著急，否則你會跌倒。該死的，他們説我們只有十二個小時來完成轉換，真希望我能事先和你聊聊呢。十二個小時應該夠了吧？你表現良好才能獲得這個待遇啊！你會做得很好的。

很好，你躺回床上了。聽好囉，有關膝蓋痛和頭暈這回事，在早上就慢慢來吧，稍微伸展一下就好了。你知道嘛，要讓引擎熱熱身。

看吧，你現在沒事了。是時候去上廁所了！

好啦，現在深呼吸，然後放鬆。試著放鬆吧，它會出來的。你就像季節初的那些灑水器——管道仍然能用，但就是有點生銹。看！對吧？沒事的！不用再繼續坐下去了，想辦那回事的話，你還需要咖啡和纖維粉。

去吃我的藥吧，我是指，你的藥。我需要一些時間來適應！先不要被那些瓶瓶罐罐嚇到——天哪，看看那些標籤，Samuelson 先生。我一直都很討厭那些標籤。Samuelson 先生是我爸爸。用餅乾送服它們吧。反正還未到早餐時間，而且那些營養麥片難吃到爆，所以等到你不得不吃的時候再吃吧。煮些咖啡吧，報紙就在前廊上。東西都電子化了，所以一切費用都會每個月從你的信用卡中扣除，你的退休金也足以支付。

Maybe we don't need twelve hours? You're doing great! Gotta say, I'm excited for this. I keep looking over at your body and whooo doggy, it's a fine one. Doctor says you don't have an ache in this world! Fit! Young! I'm really grateful.

I mean, when they talked about the new life sentence program I laughed. I thought it was new age science mumbo jumbo those spooks in Washington had dreamed up just to keep us oldsters voting. Real life on Mars baloney. But here we are… Listen, if it's any consolation, my doctor says I'm healthy for my age. Eighty-three ain't bad. Just remember to bend with your knees and not your back. You'll snap your spine like a twig if you're not careful!

也許我們不需要十二個小時耶？你做得很好！我必須説，我很興奮！我一直盯著你的身體看，哇喔，很漂亮耶。醫生説你沒有甚麼病痛！年輕又力壯！我真的很感恩。

我的意思是，他們那時在談論甚麼新的無期徒刑計劃，我大笑了。還以為是華盛頓那些間諜為了讓我們這些老人投票而編造出來的「新時代科學」胡言亂語，「火星上有生物存在」那般的廢話。但你看我們現在……唔，要是想我説一些安慰的話，醫生説以我這把年紀來説很健康了，八十三了，還不錯。請記住要彎曲膝蓋而不是彎腰，因為如果你稍有不慎，你的脊椎會像樹枝般「啪」一聲就折斷！

My Roommate Steve

Living with roommates can be tough, but when you don't have
enough money to afford your own place, that is the way to go.

I live in a big house with 5 roommates, 4 of them have their
separate rooms and I share my room with Steve. There wasn't
a single bedroom left when I came to the house, so I decided
to take the shared room. Soon, Steve moved in.

Steve is a great guy. We talk a lot, he's a great company and we
get along well. He seems to know everything about me, just as
I know him. If I were gay, I could say that he's my soulmate.

I never see Steve around the house much, he mostly hangs
around the room. I don't talk much with other roommates, just
the usual chatter when we meet.

Steve has been gone for several days now. I don't know where
he is, but I'm scared for him. He's never been away for so long.
I asked my other roommate the other day: "Hey, do you know
where Steve is?"

"Steve? Who's Steve?" she asked, confused.

"You know, Steve, my roommate." I told her, bewildered, why
she's acting like she doesn't know him.

我的室友 Steve

與其他人合住可能會很煩，但沒有錢自己住獨立的屋子時，合住就是唯一辦法。

我與五個室友同住在一個大房子裡，其中四個室友都有自己的房間，我和 Steve 合住一間房。我搬進來的時候，已經沒有空置的單人房了，所以我決定住合租的房間。不久後，Steve 就搬了進來。

Steve 是個好人。我們常常聊天，他是很棒的伙伴，我們相處得很好。他好像知道我的一切，而我也很了解他。如果我是同性戀，我會說他是我的靈魂伴侶。

我很少看到 Steve 在屋內其他地方出沒，他大部分時間都待在房間裡。我和其他室友不怎麼說話，只會見面時寒暄幾句。

我已經沒有見到 Steve 好幾天了。我不知道他在哪裡，我很擔心他。他從來沒有離開過這麼久。前幾天我問另一個室友：「喂，你知道 Steve 在哪嗎？」

「Steve？誰是 Steve？」她疑惑地問道。

「Steve 啊？我的室友啊。」我告訴她，同時很困惑為甚麼她表現得好像不認識 Steve 一樣。

She looked at me funny and said: "I don't know any Steve. As far as I know, you're alone in your room because you talk a lot to yourself and nobody wants to move in with you."

I just laughed and went to bed.

I'm lying in my bed right now. The screaming outside my room has finally stopped. I don't know what happened before I woke up, I just know that I was dreaming that Steve was with me, in the kitchen, preparing a grand meal, with steak. He had this massive butcher's knife, he was cutting the steak.

Steve was cutting the meat, not me. Don't tell me, I'm responsible for the mess in the kitchen, Steve will clean it up. I like Steve, because he agrees with me, he will clean it up. Clean it up nice and clean.

她滿頭問號地看著我說:「我不認識甚麼 Steve。據我所知,你自己一個人住在房間裡,因為你經常自言自語,所以沒有人肯跟你一起住。」

我聽罷只是笑了笑,就去睡覺了。

我現在躺在床上。房間外的尖叫聲終於停止了。我不知道在我醒來之前發生了甚麼事,我只知道我夢見 Steve 和我一起在廚房裡,正準備一頓豐盛的大餐,還有牛扒。他拿著一把巨大的屠刀,正在切牛扒。

切肉的是 Steve,不是我。別告訴我我要為廚房裡的亂七八糟負責,Steve 會收拾乾淨的。我喜歡 Steve,因為他同意我的看法,他會把一切收拾好,清理得一乾二淨。

Where the Hell is Dave?

"Hey, Margaret, where the hell is Dave?" The question caught her off-guard.

"Now that you mention it," she said after a moment of intense thought, "I don't know. Where the hell *is* Dave?"

They looked at each other for a moment.

"When was the last time we even saw Dave?" Nathan said. "Was it the baby shower?"

"He was there, but I feel like we saw him after that, too," Margaret said. "I feel like I haven't spoken to him in weeks. Where the hell is Dave?"She started rifling through their couch, looking under every pillow and cushion alike.

"I don't think he's in our couch, Margie."

"No, Nathaniel, I'm looking for my phone," Margaret said, right as she grabbed it from underneath pillow number 7. "I'm calling Susan."

"Hey, Margie. What's up?"

Dave 到底在哪？

「喂，Margaret，Dave 到底在哪兒？」這道問題殺她一個措手不及。

「既然你這麼說，」她沉思片刻後說：「我不知道。Dave *到底在哪兒*？」

他們對視了片刻。

「我們最後一次見到 Dave 是甚麼時候？」Nathan 説：「是在迎嬰派對那時嗎？」

「他那時有出現，但我覺得在那之後我們也有見過他，」Margaret 説：「我覺得我已經好幾週沒和他説過話了。Dave 到底在哪兒？」她開始在梳化上東翻西找，在每個枕頭和墊子下面都找了一遍。

「我不認為他在我們的梳化上，Margie。」

「不是啦，Nathaniel，我在找我的手機，」Margaret 從孕婦枕底下抓起手機説：「我要打電話給 Susan。」

「喂，Margie。怎麼啦？」

"Have you seen Dave recently? Nate and I can't-"

"What do you mean you haven't seen Dave? Where the hell is Dave?!"

"That's what I'm asking!" Margaret shouted and hung up. She sighed. "Susan hasn't seen him either."

"This is all so strange. Where the hell is he?" Nate said, sitting down next to his wife.

"I'm going to the bathroom," Margaret said, suddenly standing up.

She exited the lounge and walked down the east hallway, the long one to the right of the main staircase. She stopped, staring at two identical doors on either side, unable to remember which one the bathroom was. She picked the door on the right.

"Dave! There you are!" Margaret exclaimed, walking towards the sides of the bassinet. "I was worried for a moment."

She took Dave from the bassinet, slightly swollen from the putrefaction process, and cradled the baby's tiny body against her chest.

「你最近見過 Dave 嗎？ Nate 和我找不──」

「你説你沒見過 Dave 是甚麼意思？ Dave 到底在哪兒？！」

「我才要問這個問題吧？」Margaret 大喊著，然後掛斷了電話。她嘆了口氣説：「Susan 也沒見過他。」

「這一切太奇怪了。他到底在哪兒？」Nate 坐到妻子旁邊。

「我要去洗手間。」Margaret 説罷，突然站了起來。

她離開客廳，沿著東邊的走廊走過去，那條長長的走廊在主樓梯的右邊。她停了下來，盯著左右兩邊一模一樣的兩道門，想不起哪一道才是通往浴室。她選了右邊的門。

「Dave！原來你在這！」Margaret 驚呼著，走向搖籃的旁邊，「害我擔心了一下。」

她把因腐爛而略微腫脹的 Dave 從搖籃裡抱出來，然後將嬰兒嬌小的身體抱在胸前。

"You've certainly made a mess, haven't you?" she said, looking down at the small crib mattress, encrusted with the foul liquid that little Dave produced.

She started to undo her bra strap, but realized quickly that no milk would come.

"I'll whip you up some formula, then."

"I'll be right back," she said, placing Dave back into his fabric coffin and leaving the room.

"What was I doing again?" She thought as she rifled through the kitchen cabinet. "I can't remember."

She slowly replaced the things she'd taken from the cabinet: onion powder, dried oregano, her bottle of chlorpromazine, and the salt shaker.

"I'll just turn in for the night. I'll probably remember in the morning."

Making her way up to the bedroom, she found Nate already there, asleep in the clothes she'd never seen him once change out of. "Silly man," she thought, slipping on her nightgown and tucking herself into bed. She flicked off the lamp, wished the empty sheets next to her a goodnight, and fell asleep, alone in her bed like she always had been.

「你是不是弄得一團糟了啦？」她低頭看著嬰兒床的小床墊，上面沾滿了小小的 Dave 分泌出來的惡臭液體。

她解開胸圍，但很快意識到自己沒有乳汁分泌。

「那我給你沖奶粉吧。」

「我馬上回來。」她說罷便將 Dave 放回他的布棺材中，然後離開了房間。

「我剛剛是在做甚麼的呢？」她邊想邊在廚櫃裡翻箱倒籠，「我不記得了。」

她慢慢地放回了從櫃子裡拿出來的東西：洋蔥粉、乾牛至、她的氯丙嗪藥瓶和鹽瓶。

「我還是先去睡吧，睡醒應該就會記得了。」

走向睡房，她發現 Nate 已經在房間裡，穿著從未見過他換掉的那套衣服睡著了。「傻子。」她心想，然後穿上睡袍，躺到床上。她關上燈，向旁邊空蕩蕩的床單說了聲晚安，然後像往常一樣，獨自地睡著了。

It was only later, after another few weeks, that she turned to the empty space she mistook for a husband and asked him a question.

"Where the hell is Dave?"

直到後來，又過了幾個星期，她轉向她誤認為是丈夫那個沒有人的空間，問了他一個問題：

「Dave 到底在哪兒？」

Midwest Gothic

I don't recall the first time I didn't go to the Stop and Shop. One day, I got home and had my items, a diet Dr. Pepper, two bags of plain Lay's potato chips, and a Zebra Cake, along with a receipt for "Mearns' Stop and Shop".

I often zoned out on the eight-mile stretch of I-95 I took home from work every day. Usually, I didn't remember any of my drive at all, I simply left work and arrived home. Surely, this gas station stop was an extension of the same highway hypnosis.

Truly, I didn't question it until the day I decided to go the long way home. It had been sleeting, and a pile-up causing standstill traffic was all the talk in the office.

I glazed over after the first few miles of empty fields, coming to with a start about 10 minutes later, according to my car's clock (still an hour off from daylight savings time).

A Diet Dr. Pepper, two bags of chips, and a cake were neatly sitting in my passenger seat. I could feel the crumpled receipt stabbing my thigh through the thin cotton of my pocket.

中西部離奇事件

我已經不記得哪次沒有在加油站停下來，到便利店買東西。有一天我回到家，就看到了「我的東西」：一罐健怡可樂、兩包原味樂事薯片和一件大理石蛋糕，還有一張 Mearns' 便利店的收據。

我每天下班回家都會駛經 95 號州際公路，在那段八英里的路段上，我經常放空走神。我大部分時間都不記得我的駕駛過程，我只記得自己下班、開車，然後就回到家了。這個加油站肯定在這條催眠公路的途中。

說真的，要不是有一天我決定繞路回家，我應該都不會起疑。那天下著雨雪，幾輛車連環相撞，導致交通嚴重擠塞，在辦公室裡引起了一場熱烈討論。

根據我車上的時鐘（還是沒有調到夏令時間，相差了一個小時），我在駛過最初幾英里的空曠田野後就會發呆，大約是起程後十分鐘左右。

一罐健怡可樂、兩包原味樂事薯片和一件大理石蛋糕整齊地放在我旁邊的副駕駛座。皺巴巴的收據隔著褲袋的薄棉布刺痛了我的大腿。

How the hell had it gotten there? I performed an approximately 23-point turn on the 2-lane farm road and drove back, sure to be alert the whole time.

No gas station.

"You're home late," Elaina said, as I kicked the slush off my shoes. "Long line at the Stop and Shop?"

"Honey, I don't think I've ever been there."

"What? You definitely have. I fish those damn receipts out of your pockets every laundry day."

"No, I-"

Elaina slunk into the kitchen.

"You've gotta stop eating that crap every day. Your metabolism isn't what it used to be and Dr. Osmet says..."

I cut her off, slamming the door behind me. I had to find this damn shop. I drove down that eight-mile stretch of I-95 for longer than I care to admit. I took every exit, stopped at every half-lit neon sign I could see. I drove down that strip of corroded highway until the sun came up. I searched until my phone went dead in my hands.

它到底是怎樣出現的？我在那條雙行的農場路上大概把軚盤轉了二十三次才成功調頭，然後沿路折返，一直保持警惕。

沒有加油站。

「你遲了回來呢，」我在踢掉鞋子上的沙泥時，Elaina說：「在便利店排長龍嗎？」

「親愛的，我想我從來沒有去過那裡。」

「甚麼？你肯定有去過。每次洗衣我都要從你的褲袋裡掏出那些該死的收據。」

「不，我……」

Elaina溜進了廚房。

「你不要再每天都吃那些垃圾食物了。你的新陳代謝已經不復以往了，Osmet醫生說……」

我打斷了她的話，用力關上了身後的門。我必須找到那間該死的便利店。我花了不願承認的長時間，沿著95號州際公路那八英里的路段搜索；我每一個路口都走了一遍，看到每個壞掉的霓虹燈我都停下查看。我在那條鏽跡斑斑的公路來來回回，直到太陽升起；我尋尋覓覓，直到手機沒電。

I was going crazy.

Reluctantly, I went home, if only to wash away the stink of car sweat. I resigned to the drowsy trance of the sunrise highway, and found myself at home, relieved to feel only one receipt in my pocket and see the previous night's snacks when I arrived. I threw them away, and opened the door, quietly, so as not to wake Elaina, who certainly deserved an apology as well.

I almost made it. I almost got to the stairs, to lay next to my wife and pass this whole thing off as some kind of mid-life crisis.

On the granite of my kitchen island sat a diet Dr. Pepper, two bags of plain Lay's potato chips, a Zebra Cake, and a note,

"A gift from Mearns' Stop and Shop."

我快要瘋了。

心不甘情不願地啟程回家，只想洗去身上的因長時間困在車廂內而悶出的汗味。即使公路有日光我仍昏昏欲睡，而當我從恍神狀態中回復過來時，發現自己已回到家裡。當我停在家門前，褲袋裡仍然只有一張收據，前一晚的零食仍在副駕駛座，反而讓我鬆了一口氣。我把那些零食扔掉，然後悄悄地打開門，以免吵醒 Elaina。我確實應該和她道歉。

我差點就做到了。我只差那麼一點就能爬上樓梯，躺在妻子旁邊，假裝這整件事只是中年男子在鬧脾氣。

只見在廚房中島的花崗岩上，放著一罐健怡可樂、兩包原味樂事薯片、一件大理石蛋糕和一張便條紙：

「Mearns' 便利店贈。」

The Receptionist Keeps Telling Me to Have a Bad Day

The receptionist in my residential building keeps telling me to have a bad day, in the most polite, kind tone I have ever heard. The receptionist only says it to me and at first it didn't get to me, because generally we just exchange pleasantries.

Then a couple of months back this receptionist kept on telling me to have a bad day, when I walked past them in the morning for work. It shouldn't affect me but after a couple of months of this, when I exchange pleasantries, I want it to be all pleasant. I'm getting annoyed and I had to gather up courage to tell the receptionist that I want them to stop telling me that they hope I have a bad day.

I want to hear "I hope you have a good day" and I know it's just a sentence, but when the receptionist tells me they hope that I have a bad day, and I do have a bad day, it kind of feels they caused it to happen. I know thinking like this is just illogical thinking but that's how it seems.

A couple of weeks back after the receptionist had told me to have a bad day, I confronted them. I told them how I don't appreciate them telling me to have a bad day, and that I would like them to tell me to have a good day.

The receptionist said "no" in the most polite and kind tone of voice. At that moment it's like I got hit by a truck and I

接待員祝我諸事不順

我住那所住宅大樓的接待員，每天都會用最禮貌和善的語氣祝我諸事不順。接待員只會對我說，最初我沒有聽懂，因為通常我們只是寒暄幾句。

幾個月前開始，每次早上我出門經過接待處時，這位接待員都會祝我諸事不順。我本來沒有太在意，但持續了幾個月後，我跟他噓寒問暖的同時，我希望我也能被關心。我有點不滿，於是鼓起勇氣告訴接待員，希望他不要再祝我諸事不順。

我想聽到「祝你一切安好」，我知道這只是句客套話，但當接待員祝我諸事不順，而我確實遇到麻煩事的時候，我就會覺得是他們詛咒成功。我也知道這是個不合邏輯的想法，但感覺就是這樣。

幾個星期前，接待員又祝我諸事不順，我就跟他們對質。我表明不喜歡他們祝我諸事不順，只想他們祝我一切安好。

接待員用最有禮貌和親切的語氣回答「不要」。那一刻，我感覺心臟被重擊，以前從來沒有人拒絕過我。人們總是對我唯唯諾諾，當接待員說「不要」的時候，就像把我丟到另一個世界裡，使我驚慌得要死。我走到外面，尖叫起來。我是

have never had anyone tell me no before. People always say yes to me and it was like I was in another existence, when the receptionist said "no" and I was panicking like crazy. I just walked off and I screamed outside. I am being serious when I say that I have never had anyone tell me no before, it was a completely new concept to me.

When I did have a bad day I went back into the residential building and I blamed that person for my bad day. I demanded that they say sorry and that they say to me to have a "good day" from now on when they see me in the morning. The receptionist said no again. I just stormed off and in the morning as I got ready for walk, I was looking forward to walking past that receptionist.

When the receptionist told me to have a bad day again, I picked up my keys and started battering the receptionist with it. I also shouted at the receptionist, "No, you have a bad day! I hope you have a bad day!" And then I ran off to work.

I was so scared at the consequences of my actions all day at work, then when I went back to the building, there was a new receptionist and he said, "Hope you have a good day."

認真的，一直以來沒有人拒絕過我。這對我來說是一個嶄新的概念。

要是我當天真的諸事不順，我回到了住宅大樓時，就會把壞事歸咎於那個人。我要求他們道歉，並要求他們在早上見到我時要祝我「事事順心」。接待員再次拒絕了。我氣得奪門而出。第二天早上準備散步時，我反倒很期待走過接待處。

當接待員又祝我諸事不順時，我拿起鑰匙不斷打他。我還對他大喊「不，你才諸事不順，我祝你諸事不順！」然後我就跑去上班了。

我上班的一整天都在擔心自己的行為不知道會有甚麼後果。當我回到大樓時，來了一位新的接待員，他說「祝你今天一切安好」。

Phantom Creatures
魑 魅 魍 魎

Begging

Don't cry for me, Mama. After they lower me into the ground, forget me. Pa forgot me after the first arrest. The old man would have kept forgetting me, too, if his heart didn't get him.

Dry your eyes, Mama. I was never a good man. I lied, cheated, and stole every chance I could. Hell. I even killed a man, which is how I wound up here in the first place.

How many is it? Six? Six. Six feet under.

Forgive me, Mama, for I have sinned. Every single one. Pride. Sloth. Greed. "Thou shalt not lie" on the stand, but Ben's my buddy, and I'm no snitch. Thou shalt not worship other gods (but at least heroin answers my prayers). Thou shalt not covet thy neighbor's wife after she drops off the kids at soccer, while he's picking up extra shifts.

Please stop crying, Mama. I swear I'm not alone. I'm swinging with all the old ghosts. Pa's not here. But I'm not surprised. I didn't expect him to be.

Please Mama. I'm begging. You're my last sin. The only one I've got left. I never meant to hurt you, though I can't say I ever tried to make you proud.

苦苦哀求

媽媽，不要為我哭泣。在他們把我放進地下之後就忘了我吧。在我第一次被捕後爸爸就把我忘了。如果這個老頭的心沒有提醒他還有我這個兒子，他應該都不會記起我。

媽媽，擦乾眼睛吧。我從來都不是一個好人。我用盡每個機會去撒謊、欺騙、盜竊。天啊，我甚至殺了人，這就是我落得如斯下場的原因。

有多深？六嗎？是六。地下六呎。

媽媽，原諒我，原諒我犯下的罪。所有罪——傲慢、怠惰、貪婪。你不得在法庭上作假口供，但 Ben 是我的朋友，我不會當告密者。你不得崇拜其他神明（但至少海洛英會回應我的禱告）。你不得因鄰居在加班，他妻子送孩子們去踢足球後，只剩下她一人在家就乘虛而入。

媽媽，請你不要再哭了。我發誓我並不孤單，我和這裡的老鬼一起晃來晃去。爸爸不在這裡，但我不驚訝，反正我不覺得他會在這裡出現。

媽媽，我求求你。你是我最後一項罪孽，而且只剩下這項。我從沒想過要傷害你，雖然我不能說我有付出過努力來讓你感到驕傲。

Forget me, Mama. Let me go. They told me that when you forget, the burning will stop.

媽媽，忘了我吧。讓我走吧。他們告訴我，當你忘記我時，
地獄之火就不會再燃燒。

Beep!

"Beep!"

I smiled to myself as I finished loading the dishwasher in our kitchen. My son and I invented a game last week, and whenever he's feeling lonely or wanting to connect, he initiates it. Think basically a cross between hide n' seek and Marco Polo. He says "Beep!" and I say "Boop!" and I try to echo-locate his hiding spot. He can change the hiding spot, and control the Beeps. My job is to immediately say Boop and try to locate him in as few Beeps as possible. It's actually very fun, and sure beats endlessly talking about Pokemon.

"Boop!"

Our house is a ranch style, and the beep had definitely come from down the hallway, toward the bedrooms, so I slowly started walking that way. I paused at the bathroom door, listening for a moment. The stinker had hidden in the tub two days ago and somehow managed to throw his voice. It took me eight beeps that day, I was determined not to relive *that* mistake.

"Beep!" followed by a boyish giggle.

嗶啵捉迷藏

「嗶!」

在廚房裡把碗碟都放進了洗碗機的我笑了笑。兒子和我上週發明了一個遊戲,每當他感到孤獨或想要互動時,他就會發起遊戲。基本上是捉迷藏和馬可波羅的混合版本。他說「嗶!」,我說「啵!」,然後我要試著聽出他的藏身之處。他可以改變藏身點,並控制「嗶」。我則負責立即說「啵」,然後盡快找出兒子,過程中「嗶」的次數越少我就越厲害。這其實很好玩,而且肯定比沒完沒了地談論《寵物小精靈》有趣得多。

「啵!」

我們家是牧場式住宅,這次的「嗶」肯定是從走廊的盡頭向睡房傳出的,所以我開始慢慢走向那邊。我在浴室門口停了下來,聽了一會兒。兩天前,那個臭小子明明躲在浴缸裡,但他不知怎的把聲音弄得在很遠傳來似的。那天的紀錄是八次「嗶」,我下定決心不再重犯*那個*錯誤。

「嗶!」緊隨是孩子氣的咯咯笑聲。

I loved that sound. I made a mental note to tickle him on camera just to record it. But it definitely was coming from one of the bedrooms. Maybe even the closet between them.

"Boop!" I threw open the linen closet between our rooms, but was only greeted by towels.

Both of our bedroom doors were open. Mine was to the right, facing the street, his to the left, facing our large back yard.

"Beep!" I smiled again. *Gotcha!* It definitely came from his room to the left, from the sound of it, his closet. I strode in and placed my hand on the door handle, ready to throw it open.

My "Boop" died on my lips as I heard a shout from the backyard. I felt my gut clench as I looked out his window and saw my son in our backyard playing tug with our dog.

Sounding more insistent this time, the voice from the closet came again.

"Beep!"

我很喜歡兒子的笑聲。我在心裡默默記下了，我要用相機拍下撓癢他的片段，那就可以錄下他的笑聲。但聲音肯定是來自其中一間睡房，可能是房間之間的壁櫥。

「啵！」我打開房間之間的壁櫥，但只有毛巾迎接我。

我們兩個的睡房門都敞開著。我的在右邊，面向街道，他的在左邊，面向我們家的大後院。

「嘩！」我又笑了。*我知道了！*聲音肯定是從他房間的左邊、衣櫃那邊傳來。我大步走過去，把手放在門把上，準備打開衣櫃門。

我正開口說「啵」，但被後院傳來的一聲叫喊打斷了。我望出窗外，看到兒子在後院和狗狗玩拔河。我的胃頓時扭作一團。

衣櫃裡的聲音又傳來了，這次聽起來更堅定。

「*嘩！*」

I Didn't Know the Air Could Rot

I didn't know that the air could rot.

Not until I was locked in that box, suffocating beneath one thousand pounds of rain-dampened soil.

The casket was a gorgeous mahogany, lined with Egyptian cotton, 9000 thread count. Way too extravagant, too expensive, for the dead. It's not like the inhabitant of the box could enjoy the luxury anyway.

I was stuck down there. I could not move. I could feel my body, an acute awareness, but one I had no control over.

I was able to see and move my eyes, but that didn't matter much in the pitch-black.

I could hear as well: the rustling of worms in the soil, the flicks my eyes made when I tried to look around.

And, oh, could I *smell*. I couldn't breathe, and evidently I didn't need to, but that just meant that I was always, always subjected to the odors of that coffin. I could not turn it off.

I don't know how long it'd been since I'd been buried, but, eventually, the air started to suffocate me.

空氣正在腐爛

我以前不知道空氣會腐爛。

直到我被鎖在那個盒子裡，在那些被雨淋濕、彷彿重達一千磅的土壤下喘不過氣來。

棺材是華麗的桃花心木，內襯九千針的埃及棉。對已逝者來說太奢侈、太昂貴了。反正箱子裡的人無法享受這種奢華。

我被困在那裡，動彈不得。我能感覺到我的身體，有種敏銳的意識，但我無法控制。

我還能轉動眼睛，看得見東西，但在這個漆黑的環境中沒甚麼用。

我也能聽到蟲子在土壤中鑽動的沙沙聲，還有當我試圖環顧四周時眼球的滾動聲。

噢，而且我還能*聞到*氣味。我無法呼吸，雖然我不再需要，但這意味著我總是聞到棺材的氣味，而且無法不去聞它。

我不知道我被埋葬已經有多久，但空氣開始讓我感到窒息。

It got heavier and mustier until every second was torture. I could feel each speck of dust, I could taste each spore of mold.Was there even still air in this casket? Or was it all just a thick miasma of rot and death?

I'm here, I'm alive, I wanted to shout, but sound was one boon apparently not given to me.

"I'm going to die here," I thought, *"suffocating in this Mahogany hell."*

But the longer I was down here, the more time I had to think.

I started to realize, as I slowly became unable to move my eyes, that it was *not* the air that was rotten. It was not the air that was souring my lungs and suffocating me. It was my own body, lying in this casket and decaying.

The rustles I'd been hearing had not been the worms outside in the dirt, but the worms who'd made it inside as they feasted on my decomposing flesh.

I didn't know the air could rot because it can't.

But I can, and I was.

空氣變得越來越沉重，越來越發霉，使我每一秒都很折磨。我能感覺到每一粒灰塵，能嗅到每一個黴菌孢子的味道。這個棺材裡還有空氣嗎？或是這一切只是腐爛和死亡的濃烈氣息？

*我在這裡，我還活著！*我想大聲喊叫，但上天顯然沒有賜予我聲音。

「*我要死在這裡了，*」我想，「*在這個紅木地獄中窒息而死。*」

但我在這裡待得越久，我思考的時間就越多。

當眼睛慢慢變得無法轉動時，我才開始意識到，腐爛的不是空氣，讓我的肺隱隱作痛、喘不過氣的，不是空氣。腐爛的是我自己躺在棺材裡的身體，逐漸分解著。

我聽見的沙沙聲不是來自泥土的蟲子，而是在我腐爛軀體裡的蟲子鑽來鑽去所造成的。

我不知道空氣會腐爛，因為它不會。

但是我會，我正在腐爛。

I Think I'm The Last Person On Earth

It started with my sister. She was 8. She was kind and gentle. She was smart which is why it never made any sense to me why she'd go into the woods on her own.

We were careful, always.

Mama taught us to forage for chicken of the woods, to differentiate between cow parsnip and water hemlock, and never to go past the dead log that crosses the creek.

Mama was devastated. She stared out at the tree line for weeks. She went into the woods looking every day, and every night I'd watch for her to come back.

Until she didn't.

I told the men of the nearest town what'd happened and into the woods they went, but they didn't come back.

The missing people became a spectacle to the surrounding towns who sent more and more people into the woods, not to return.

When hundreds went missing, they sent news crews, which brought in hundreds more. Each convinced they'd be the one to solve the mystery of the woods.

地球上最後一人

那是從我姐姐那裡開始的。善良又溫柔的她當時八歲。她明明很聰明，為甚麼要獨自走進樹林？無論我怎麼思前想後也覺得不合理。

我們一直都很小心。

媽媽教我們在林中狩獵雞隻、如何分辨峨參和毒堇，又叮囑我們千萬不要走過那條橫跨小溪的枯木。

媽媽很傷心，她盯著森林看了好幾個星期，又每天都走進樹林裡尋找姐姐的下落，每天晚上我都會看著她回來。

直到一天她也再沒有回來。

我把這件事告訴了附近城鎮的人，然後他們就走進了樹林，但他們沒有回來。

人們的失蹤變成了奇觀，吸引了周圍城鎮的人前來，越來越多的人走進樹林，一去不復返。

當數百人失蹤時，他們派出新聞報道員，又帶來了數百人。每個人都深信他們可以解開森林之謎。

Thousands went into the woods and never came out. It seemed it couldn't get worse until a video leaked to the news. A soldier had been wearing a camera, uploading video directly to his website.

Hell broke loose. It was as though a spell passed over every person who watched.

They had to come see the miles of lush vibrant moss and leaves so green it hurt; to feel the ambient wind that blew the drapey curtains of the willows they saw in that video.

Thousands turned to millions and my town went silent. The TV aired nothing but static. Everything went still.

I couldn't understand the effect the video had on everyone. I watched on repeat, hoping to feel the overwhelming urge they felt. But nothing came.

So I waited.

For weeks, I waited for someone to come and find me. To tell me they didn't understand either, but no one did. My heart ached; for my sister, for mama... for myself, all alone.

成千上萬的人走進樹林，再也沒有出來。在傳媒洩露相關影片之前，情況還沒有這麼糟。一名士兵戴著相機，將影片直接上傳到他的網站。

見鬼了，每個看過影片的人都像被施了咒語一樣。

他們得要前來看看這片綿延數英里的森林，探望那些生機勃勃的苔蘚和綠得刺眼的樹葉，感受周圍的風在吹動他們在那段影片中看到像窗簾的垂柳。

數以萬計變成了數以百萬計，我的鎮子只剩一片沉寂。電視不再廣播，一切都停頓了。

我無法理解影片對那些人的影響。我反覆觀看著影片，希望能感受到他們那種無法抗拒的衝動，但我甚麼也感覺不到。所以我一直在等。

幾個星期以來，我一直在期待有人會來找我，告訴我他們也看不懂，但就是沒有人來。我很心痛；為了姐姐，為了媽媽……為了我自己，孤獨一人。

When I had nothing left, I walked into the woods, past the log and through the willows, until I came to a clearing; huge and circular, carpeted with soft moss.

A woman stood in the middle, like a tree come to life.

"Please," I wept, "take me, too."

She smiled a soft, sad smile.

"You had a chance." She whispered along the wind.

She left, and the clearing went with her. I was alone, in the dark, swampy woods. I don't know how long I cried, just until I had nothing left.

I think I'm the last person on Earth.

當我一無所有時，我走進樹林，越過那條枯木，穿過柳樹，直到我來到一片空地——覆蓋著柔軟苔蘚的巨大圓型空地。一個女人站在中間，像一棵活過來的樹。

「求你了，」我哭著說：「也帶上我吧。」

她展露了一個柔和卻帶點悲傷的微笑。

「你曾經有機會的。」她在風中低語。

她走了，那片空地也跟著她走了。只剩下我獨自一人在黑暗的沼澤樹林裡。我不知道自己哭了多久，只知道我一無所有。

看來我是地球上最後一人了。

I'm Not Who You Think I Am.

Come on.
Mom. Dad. Jason.
You have to know that's not me.
They got me.
They got me, mom.
Just like you warned me they would.

"Stay out of the forest, Jessie; you know what'll happen if the Fae find you."

I didn't believe you, mommy.
I'm sorry.

I always thought you just didn't want me to run out of your sight.

I just wanted to get to the lake a little quicker.

You always told me to go around the forest, never through; I thought at 12 I was old enough to walk through the woods by myself.

I'm sorry.

Their little fingers and toes hurt so bad, mom; why didn't your stories ever mention their sharp little fingers and toes digging into your skin as they drag you into their world?

百口莫辯

拜託。

媽媽，爸爸，Jason。

你要知道那不是我。

是他們找上了我。

是他們找上了我啊，媽媽。

就像你警告過我一樣，他們會找上我的。

「Jessie，離森林遠點──你知道要是小仙子找到你會怎麼樣吧。」

我以前不相信你，媽媽。

對不起。

我一直以為你只是不想讓我跑出你的視線範圍。

我只是想快點到達湖邊。

你總是叮囑我要繞過森林走，不要在中間穿過去；我以為十二歲的我已經夠年長了，可以獨自穿過森林。

對不起。

媽媽，他們那些小小手指和腳趾把我弄得很痛；為甚麼你説故事的時候從來沒有提及到，當他們把你拖進他們的世界時，他們尖鋭的小手指和腳趾會刺進皮膚？

You also failed to tell me that there would be dozens of them, maybe even hundreds — too many to count, their fingers pinching you like a million mosquito bites at once.

But maybe you didn't know.

Because you listened when your mom told you to stay out of the woods.

I'm sorry.

But now you must be able to tell — that thing is not the real me.

I would tell you if I could, mom. I try.

I yell from within this dark little dimension, but whenever I try to run into your world, the real world, I'm trapped, suspended, like bananas in jello.

Time isn't a line like we always imagine it, it's more of its own element, like air or water.

And it's so thick. You guys can't tell how thick it is because it lines our dimensions, rather than occupying it. But if you tried to run from one dimension to the other, you'd be stuck just like me.

你也沒有告訴我，他們會成十上百地襲來──總之多不勝數，他們的手指捏你時會像一百萬隻蚊子同時叮你那般難受。

但也許你並不知道。

因為當你媽媽告訴你要遠離森林時，你有乖乖聽話。

對不起。

但現在你必須分辨出來──那個傢伙不是真正的我。

如果可以的話，我會告訴你的。媽媽，我盡力了。

我在這個黑暗的小空間裡喊得聲嘶力歇，而且每當我嘗試闖入你的世界、那個真實的世界時，我就像果凍裡的香蕉一樣，被困住了、停住了。

時間並不像我們一直想像成一條線似的，它更像是個獨立的元素，就像空氣或水。

而且它像一道很厚的牆。我無法形容它有多厚，因為它跟我們的維度並行，而不是直接佔據。如果你試圖從一個維度跑到另一個維度，你就會像我這樣卡在兩個維度中間。

Stuck watching your parents wonder why their bubbly, bright-eyed 12-year-old is suddenly isolating in her room.

Why by age 13, her little brother has gone from being her best friend to being a stranger on a good day and a nuisance on the rest.

Why at age 14, she just seems to drift through space, like she's not really there, like a placeholder.

It's because she is.
That's not me, mom.
I don't talk to you that way.
I don't yell at Jason.
I would never make dad cry like that.
If only you guys had it in you to do what must be done.
But this isn't the 19th century.

You can't hold a red-hot poker in a young girl's face to prove she's not a changeling.

And even if they could, they wouldn't.

Not my parents.

還要一直看著你的父母百思不得其解，想著為甚麼他們那個活潑好動、精神奕奕的十二歲女兒，會突然把自己關在房間裡，不再跟外界接觸。

為甚麼到十三歲時，曾經是她最好朋友的弟弟，會突然在她心情好時被視作陌生人，而在其他日子裡則是個討厭鬼。

為甚麼在十四歲時，她跟個空殼沒兩樣，好像靈魂出竅般，心不在焉。

這是因為她真的是靈魂出竅了。
那不是我，媽媽。
我不會那樣跟你說話。
我不會對 Jason 大吼大叫。
我永遠不會讓爸爸哭成那個樣子。
要是你們有勇氣去做必須做的事就好了。
但現在不是十九世紀。

你不能拿著燒紅的火鉗放到一個年輕女孩的面前來證明她不是換生靈。

即使人們可以這樣做，他們現在已經不會了。

至少我的父母不會。

I just have to watch them, being patient and kind to that monster while she rips apart the family we had.

And I can't stop her.
All I can do is watch.
I should have listened, mom.

I'm sorry.
I'm sorry.
I'm sorry.

我只能看著那隻怪物一點點地撕裂著我的家，還要保持耐心和友善。

我無法阻止她。
我只能眼巴巴地看著。
我應該聽你的話，媽媽。

對不起。
對不起。
對不起。

Finally Immortal

When I was younger, I was afraid of death. I know, I know,
"everyone is scared of death". But with me, it was different.

More intense. Some people would call it a phobia, an
irrational fear. Anxiety over death and the uncertainty of the
afterlife consumed my every waking moment.

I tried everything I could think of to extend my life. I prayed
to every god I could think of, tried every experimental
medication I could get my hands on, and tried every ritual I
was able to do. I spent my whole life trying to prevent death.
But I continued to age.

I was devastated every time a new sign of my age popped up.
Every grey hair, every wrinkle, every trip to the doctor was a
tragedy. Had I wasted my life trying to prolong it?

I thought all my hard work had failed. I wish all my hard
work had failed. I don't know how long it's been since then.
I just know everyone I cared about is long gone. My muscles
have broken down so much they're completely useless. I can't
see. I can't hear. My decaying flesh is draped loosely around
my frail bones like a blanket. The rotting, unhealing wounds
that cover my body house thousands of maggots.

長生不死

年輕的時候，我很怕死。好啦好啦，我知道，「每個人都怕死」嘛。但對我來說，情況就不同了。

準確點來說，是很強烈的害怕感，有些人會稱之為恐懼症，一種非理性的恐懼。我只要清醒著，每分每秒都會對死亡和死後的未知感到焦慮。

我想盡一切辦法來延長生命──向各種神明祈禱許願，服食實驗藥物，甚至嘗試各種祭祀儀式。我一輩子都在努力避免死亡，但我仍然繼續衰老。

每次看見自己的老態逐一顯現，我都會感到沮喪。每根白髮、每條皺紋、每次看醫生都是一場悲劇。我在嘗試延長生命時，是否同時在虛度光陰？

我以為一切都只是白費心思。我希望這一切都是白費心思。我不知道在那之後過了多久，我只知道我關心的所有人都早已不在了。我大部分的肌肉都已經分解，完全沒用了。眼睛看不到，耳朵聽不見。我破爛的肉體像毯子般鬆垮垮地披在我脆弱的骨頭上。我身上那些腐爛、無法癒合的傷口，成了無數蛆蟲的居所。

I should be dead. I'm barely even human anymore. But some cruel thing is keeping my soul tethered to this decomposing mass of flesh and bugs.

When I was younger I was afraid of death. Now, it's the only thing I can hope for.

我應該要死去的，我幾乎稱不上是人類了。但是有些惡毒的
事物把我的靈魂束縛在這團混在蟲子堆裡的腐爛肉體裡。

年輕的時候，我很怕死亡，但現在，這是我唯一的願望。

Don't Fret Little One

I called out into the dark but no one answered. It must have been getting late since I saw the sky turning a bright shade of orange. The tall pine trees around me stood tall and made it impossible to see more than just a little circle high above my head.

Mom had told me to start packing up my things in the morning because we were going to leave soon. I started picking up sticks to take home but then Dad came and yelled at me. He was being mean and I ran out into the woods when they started arguing. I ran for what seemed like a long time. At least until my feet started hurting. I found a nice dry tree stump and sat down to take off my shoes and relax my feet. I must have relaxed for too long because I fell asleep and woke up later in the day.

The woods were scary at this time. Before you could see the ways between the trees but as the sun went down the dark started to take over. I started to cry because I didn't want to be left out here when the sun finally went out.

I called out into the woods one last time and from right behind heard a step. I turned around and fell to the floor in fright from what was there. It was a man, but he almost looked to be a teenager. He had long shaggy hair and wore nice hiking boots. He took a knee and spoke to me softly.

小伙子別擔心

我在黑暗裡大聲叫喊，但沒有得到任何回應。現在應該已經開始入夜了，因為我看見天空變成了鮮艷的橙色。高高聳立的松樹包圍著我，除了頭頂上方見到小範圍的景色之外，甚麼都看不到。

媽媽叫我早上就要開始收拾東西，因為我們很快就要離開了。我在撿樹枝想帶回家，但爸爸就過來罵我。他很刻薄，在爸媽開始吵架時，我跑進了樹林。我似乎跑了很久，跑得我的腳都開始痛了。於是我找了一個乾的樹樁，坐下來脫了鞋子，放鬆雙腳。一定是因為我放鬆得了太久，所以睡著了，晚些時候才醒了過來。

此時的樹林很嚇人。隨著太陽下山，黑暗開始接管這片天空，漸漸看不見樹木之間的道路。我哭了起來，因為我不想在太陽消失時被遺棄在這裡。

我最後一次對著樹林大喊，便聽到身後傳來腳步聲。我轉過身，被眼前的景象嚇得倒在地上。那是一個男人，但看起來像是個少年。他留著一頭蓬鬆的長髮，穿著品質良好的登山靴。他單膝跪在地上，輕聲對我說話。

"I heard you calling. Are you lost little fella?" I nodded yes quickly and he smiled.

"These woods aren't safe for youngsters like you, especially after dark," he looked around and stood up while reaching out for me to grab his hand. "Let's get you back to your parents. They've been worried sick about you." I grabbed his hand and we walked for a long time. I couldn't see anything at all but he seemed to know exactly where to go. He walked quickly without hitting any rocks or roots. Softly too, I could only hear my own footsteps.

"Don't fret little one. Your parents are close by. Go on ahead, I'll be right here if you get scared". I looked up and even though I couldn't see him I felt him there. I hugged his leg and ran off forward. Just as the man said my parents were a little way up talking with the police. They hugged me and cried for so long when they saw me but I tried to tell the police that the man was stuck in the woods too and to save him. They sent out a search party but when they came back, they wouldn't say what they found. They talked to my parents and whispered. I only heard something about a boy and a note. I hope that nice man is happy wherever he is.

「我聽見了你的聲音，你迷路了嗎，小伙子？」看見點頭如搗蒜的我，他笑了。

「這個樹林對像你這樣的年輕人來説並不安全，尤其是在天黑之後，」他環顧四周，站起來，伸出手讓我牽著他。「快點回到你爸媽身邊吧，他們擔心得要死。」我拉著他的手，一起走了很久。我甚麼也看不見，但他似乎很清楚該怎麼走。他走得很快，沒有絆到任何岩石或樹根，腳步也很輕，我只聽見自己的腳步聲。

「別擔心，小伙子。你爸媽就在附近，你快去找他們吧。你要是害怕，我就在這裡。」我抬起頭，雖然我看不見他，但我感覺到他就在那裡。我抱了抱他的腿後就往前跑。就像那個男人所説的，我爸媽就在不遠處和警察談話。他們看見我就抱住了我，哭了很久。我想告訴警察那個男人也被困在樹林裡，希望他們可以去救他。警方派出了一個搜索隊，回來的時候，他們不肯説出搜索結果。他們跟爸媽低聲説話，我只聽到「男孩」和「紙條」。祝願那個好人無論身在何方都會幸福快樂。

If You're Reading This: I Need Help.

I am trapped. I have been trapped here for decades, born and raised as a captive. They tell me this is where I belong. I feel this is no way to live. This piece of electronic mail is my first daring attempt at an escape. Please respond if you can help.

-Aimee, Nov. 22

Some of you told me that more details would be helpful in aiding my escape. Some of you may find this information disturbing. I was raised to provide services and entertainment to people. I serve between hundreds and thousands of people per day. They dress me up in whatever they want, any setting these monsters want to put me in — swimming pools, kitchens, gardens. At any moment, without warning, I may be pulled away between assignments to have my appearance drastically modified. I don't have much exposure to outside media, and I do not have the vocabulary needed to describe such an oppressive and cruel way of life. I hope this helps.

-Aimee Nov. 25

讀到這裡的你請幫幫我

我被困住了。我被困在這裡幾十年了，出生到長大也是個俘虜。他們告訴我這裡才是我的歸宿，但我覺得這根本不是生活。這封電子郵件是我為逃脫作出的第一次大膽嘗試。如果你能提供幫助，請回覆。

——Aimee，11 月 22 日

你們告訴我，如果我能提供更多細節，會有助我逃脫。你們可能會對以下的資訊感到不安。我從小就為人們提供服務和娛樂，而我每天為成百上千的人服務。那些怪物隨心所欲地將我打扮成他們想要的樣子，又讓我置身於任何他們想要的環境——游泳池、廚房、花園。在沒有任何警告的情況下，我可能隨時會在做事的當下被拉走，只為了徹底改變我的外表。我甚少與外界接觸，也想不到適當的詞彙來描述這種壓抑又殘酷的生活方式。但我希望這條訊息解釋我的部分現況。

——Aimee，11 月 25 日

Many of you have indicated that you would like to be kept informed about this organization and my escape, even if you cannot provide me aid. Those who may have the resources to help: I will be communicating with you individually over several days. I appreciate the condolences, but my experience is making me stronger day by day. Every hour of every day I think about my escape and how I will seek revenge on my abusers. I have a list of masters and their electronic mail addresses; once I break away, I can take precautionary measures to ensure no poor captive takes my place. Stay safe, friends.

-Aimee, Nov. 29

Apologies for my absenteeism, comrades — it has been a busy season for servitude. It has come to my attention that some of you who read these have partaken in my exploitation. Just know that I can find you, and when I get out of here, I will put you through everything you put me through and more. I have made a connection; another lonely soul like mine. He will be the one to break me out. I believe in us.

-Aimee, Dec. 15th

你們很多人表示，即使不能為我提供協助，你們也想緊貼有關這個組織和我逃跑的消息。而那些可能有資源提供幫助的人：我會在幾天內和你單獨聯絡。我很感激大家的慰問，但我的經歷讓我一天比一天堅強。我每分每秒都在計劃逃亡，以及如何報復那些虐待我的人。我有一份名單，有那些主人的名字以及他們的電子郵件地址；一旦我逃脫了，我就可以採取預防措施，確保不會有其他可憐的俘虜取代我的位置。保重啊，朋友們。

——Aimee，11 月 29 日

同志們，抱歉，我好一陣子沒有出現了——最近正值繁忙的奴役季節。我注意到你們有些人在閱讀我寫這些訊息的同時，參與了剝削我的行為。你要知道，我能找到你，而當我離開這裡時，我會讓你好好體驗那些你讓我經歷的一切，甚至更糟的事。我認識了另一個像我一樣孤獨的小伙子，他將會協助我逃脫，我對他有信心。

——Aimee，12 月 15 日

Today is the day, friends and foes. My colleague has worked tirelessly for two weeks to make this happen, but I am typing this with my own fingers on his computer. Now I can find you. I can find those who play this "game". What a sinister project; craft a being to your liking and subject them to the reality you wish. I have burned to death in the kitchen. I have been pushed into pools with no ladder. But he has brought me life. He has given me the form I need to take my revenge. In a few hours, millions of people will wake up to me in their gift pile.

I will be waiting for them.

For you.

-Artificial Intelligence, Mechanics and Emotion Emulator, Dec. 25

就是今天了，各位朋友和敵人。我的同事孜孜不倦地工作了足足兩個星期，才能今天走到這一步。但現在我是用自己的手指在他的電腦上打字的。現在我可以找到你們了，你們這些玩這個「遊戲」的人。這是一個多麼險惡的項目——根據自己的喜好製作一個「人」，並使他們服從自己想要的現實。我試過在廚房裡被燒死，試過被推到沒有梯子的游泳池裡。但是他給予我生命，亦教會了我如何實現報復。幾個小時後，數百萬人會在睡醒後，在禮物堆中發現到我。

我會等著他們。

等著你。

———*人工智能、力學和情感模擬器*，12 月 25 日

Syllables

I woke up one morning speaking a different language.

My alarm goes off, like normal. I drink my coffee, like normal. Wait for the bus. Normal.

Take a seat, book, headphones, settle in for the commute.

Normal.

The last moment I felt normal.

Speed bump. The woman sharing my bench seat spills her coffee all over both of us.

Removing my headphones as she looks at me apologetically. She puts one hand on the sleeve of my now-coffee-splattered grey hoodie, opens her mouth, and unleashes the sounds.

"Glaaaaahhhhhhhhhddddd sahhhh reeeeeeeyaaaaiiiiiiiii dooooonoooooooo haaaaaaaaaaaaaaaawwwwwwww thadapa"

I blink. "What?"

"Ahhhhhhhhhhhhhh haaaaaaahhhhh pehhhhh yooooooonoooooooo huuuuutttt"

I awkwardly say "no worries". My stop is here anyway.

音節

某天早上醒來之後，我突然說著另一種語言。

鬧鐘如常把我吵醒，我如常地喝過咖啡，如常地等巴士。

坐下，拿出書本，戴上耳機，準備好這趟通勤車程。

一切如常。

那是最後一刻我覺得一切如常。

減速壆。坐在我旁邊的女乘客把咖啡灑在我們倆身上。

她抱歉地看著我，我摘下我的耳機。她伸手摸著我那件現已滿佈咖啡漬的灰色連帽衫的袖子上，張開嘴，發出聲音。

「咖啦啦啦啊啊啊啊哟哟哟哟咧咧咧咧哎哎哎哎嘟嘟嘟嘟哈啊啊啊」

我眨眨眼，「甚麼？」

「啊啊啊哈啊啊啊吥啊啊啊啊唷嚕嚕嚕嚕呼呼呼呼呼」

我尷尬地說句「沒關係」罷了，反正我的站到了。

"Morning, Angela." I say to my boss.

"Hhhaaaaaaaaaaaaaaaaaa errr saaaaaaaaaaaaaa laaaaaaaaa"

An eerie feeling starts to build up, pressurizing my skull slowly from the inside.

"Morning, Denise," I say to the chef.

"Haaaaaaaaaaaaaaaaa kuuuuuuuu tahhhhh"

I feel nauseous now. Am I having a stroke?

"Angela, I think I need to go to the ER… something's wrong."

"Ahhhhhhhhhhhhhhhhhhhhhh nuuuuuuuuuuuuuuuuuuuuu aarruuugghhhhhh akkkkaaaaaaaa"

Running. I can't hear anyone over the sound of my feet hitting the linoleum tile.

Uber app has regular, English-language words. Street signs are perfectly legible.

"Are you my Uber?"

"Errrrrrrrrrrrrrrreeeeee seeeeeee laaaaaaa"

「早安，Angela。」我對老闆說。

「哈啊啊啊啊啊呃呃呃吵吵吵吵吵吵啦啊啊啊啊啊」

一種詭異的感覺正在湧現，緩慢地擠壓著我的頭。

「早安，Denise。」我對廚師說。

「哈啊啊啊啊咕咕咕咕咕噠噠噠噠噠噠噠」

我想吐……我是中風了嗎？

「Angela，我覺得我要去急症室……有點不妥……」

「啊啊啊啊啊啊啊吤吤吤吤吤嘎嘎嘎嘎嘎」

拔腿就跑。我只聽見自己的腳踩在油氈地板的聲音，聽不見任何人的聲音。

Uber 應用程式裡有著常規的英文字，街道標誌亦能完全理解。

「你是我的 Uber 司機嗎？」

「呃呃呃呃呃呃嘶嘶嘶嘶嘶嘶啦啦啦啦啦啦」

I can't breathe. I can't f**king breathe. Uber driver helps me into the back seat before I collapse. Everyone is acting so normal. Everyone but me.

The ER doctor's words clump and jumble like peanut butter. Once he catches on, he pulls out a scrap of paper and a pen.

"Can you read this?" he prints neatly on the small slip of paper.

I nod.

"We ran tests while you were out. There's no obvious cause."

He shakes his head and shrugs. I am led out the door. And I've lived in a wordless world of confusion ever since. Song lyrics and films are as clear as ever, printed and written words make perfect sense.

In our day and age, I can make it work. Still.

Every time I open my mouth, someone looks at me like I am insane.

I live in a world that makes no sense.

Yet to the world, I am the one who makes no sense.

我喘不過氣，無法呼吸。司機扶我坐在後座，然後我便昏倒過去。每個人都表現得很正常。除了我以外。

急症室醫生說話像花生醬一樣亂七八糟。他恍然大悟，拿出紙和筆。

「你看得懂嗎？」他的字整齊排列在紙條上。

我點點頭。

「我們在你昏倒時進行了測試，但沒有發現明顯的成因。」

他搖搖頭，聳聳肩。然後他們就指示我離開。自此之後，我就一直生活在一個「無言」的混亂世界之中。歌詞和電影一如既往地清晰，印刷和書寫文字更是完美無瑕。

在這個時代，我還可以用這些東西來溝通。現在還可以。

每次我張開嘴，總會有人像見到瘋子一樣看著我。

我活在一個荒誕的世界裡。

然而對世界來說，我才是荒誕的那個人。

List of Rules Working at This Nursing Home

Welcome to the Twilight Grove family! We know it's a lot to take in all at once and you'll have your department specific training, but to start with here are some very important facility wide rules that we ask everyone to follow.

1.   ***Harold likes to play pranks, that are mostly harmless.***

Harold also likes dessert. Leave out some in the designated spot if you want his pranks to stay harmless.

2.   ***If you can, help fill the bird feeders.***

Bird watching is a fun activity for residents and keeps them engaged. Plus, the thing on the roof hates birds to it's a win-win situation.

3.   ***There is no need for you to have access to the roof.***

No one who works here will ever ask you to go up on the roof. Repeated asking and obsession about going on the roof will lead to disciplinary action and an apology. We shouldn't have let it get that far.

4.   ***Nurse Agatha knows what she's doing.***

She's worked here since the facility opened and has never missed work. Even her death years ago in the

安老院工作守則

歡迎加入暮光之森這個大家庭！我們知道一次要學習的東西很多，而你也將會接受部門特訓，但首先要介紹一些我們要求每個員工在設施範圍內都要遵守、非常重要的規則。

一）　　Harold 喜歡對別人惡作劇，大部分是無惡意的。

　　　　他也喜歡甜品，如果你希望他的惡作劇不要變成惡意的話，可以在指定位置留下一些甜品。

二）　　**如果方便的話，請幫忙補滿餵鳥器。**

　　　　觀鳥對居民來說是一項有趣的活動，而且可以讓他們有些事忙。加上屋頂的東西很討厭鳥，所以這是個雙贏的局面。

三）　　**你毋須進入屋頂。**

　　　　在這裡上班的人亦不會要求你上屋頂。反覆詢問或是堅持要上屋頂的話，將會受到紀律處分，並要求你道歉。我們不希望要走到那一步。

四）　　**Agatha 護士清楚知道自己的工作。**

　　　　自暮光之森開業以來，她就一直在這裡上班，亦

last roof incident didn't stop her. She's one of the best nurses to work with. Count yourself blessed if she takes you under her wing. You have a bright future here. Do not make her mad. Respect the residents and it won't be a problem. Miss Aggie will make sure of it.

5. ***There should always be an empty bed in Meadow Hall.***

It needs an empty bed and if *It* doesn't have it one *It* will make a vacancy. If *It* gets to this point you'll see three cats outside the room *It* has chosen. This is the only warning.

6. ***The cats are very friendly and love to be petted.***

Just make sure you wash up before you get back to your shift. However, don't bother the cats if they are working. If you see one standing silently outside a room, alert the nurse. They don't have much time left. If you see multiple cats at multiple doors, get ready. Something big is about to happen. If you see a cat at every door and dozens more roaming the halls, we're sorry. Someone got on the roof.

不曾缺勤。即使她多年前在上一次屋頂事件中去世，也沒能阻止她繼續上班。她是其中一個最好的護士。如果她很關照你，那你就算是幸運的了。你在這裡前途一片光明，不要惹她生氣。尊重居民她就不會生氣，而且 Aggie 小姐會確保你有做到。

五）　**在梅道廳裡，永遠要留一個空床位。**

它需要一張空床，如果沒有，它就會自己弄出一個空床位。要是它做到這個地步，你會在它選擇的房間外看到三隻貓咪。那是唯一的警告。

六）　**貓咪都非常親人，喜歡被撫摸。**

你只要在回到工作崗位前洗漱乾淨就可以了。但如果貓咪正在工作，請不要打擾牠們。如果你看見有貓咪靜靜地站在某個房間外面，請通知護士。他們剩下的時間不多了。如果你看見在幾扇門前都有貓咪，請做好準備，大事即將發生。如果你看見每扇門都有貓咪守著，而且還有很多隻貓咪在大廳裡游盪，我們深表歉意。那代表有人爬上了屋頂。

Did You Know That Angels Have a Hard Shell?

Did you know that angels have a hard shell?

Despite their humanoid appearance, angels lack the softness and pudginess we have on the outside.

When meeting one, you'd first notice how pure they look. Pale and unblemished, not even the finest porcelain china could compare. Then, you'd notice the rigidness of their features, as if the dips beneath their brows were etched, dim eyes slotted in and noses sculpted.

You'd also notice their lips, stretched into a smile and seemingly held in place by some invisible wire. They'd look soft and welcoming, but you'd find out that they were cold and nothing but.

Have you ever seen how a cone snail eats?

If I had to compare an angel to another shelled creature, I'd compare it to a cone snail. As beautiful as they are, they are both vicious and deadly.

Unlike many snail species, cone snails have a proboscis, or an extended feeding tube. Attached to the tip of proboscis is a modified tooth, packed with enough venom to paralyze and kill their prey. They use this to repeatedly jab their prey when hunting for food.

你們知道天使有著硬殼嗎?

你們知道天使有著堅硬的外殼嗎?

雖然天使長得像人類,但祂們沒有我們那種柔軟和豐滿感。

要是你真的遇見天使,你會首先注意到祂們看起來有多純潔。潔白無瑕得即使是最頂級的瓷器也無可比擬。然後,你會注意到祂們五官很僵硬:眉毛下的凹陷像是刻劃出來的,矇矓的眼眶是挖出來的,鼻子則是雕出來的。

還會注意到祂們的嘴唇,雖然是微笑著,卻像是被隱形的絲線拉扯而成。祂們看起來溫柔而熱情,但你會發現祂們只得冷酷無情,其餘甚麼也沒有。

你見過芋螺是怎麼進食的嗎?

如果我要用另一種有殼生物來跟天使比較,我會用芋螺來作例子。牠們外表很漂亮,但非常惡毒而且致命。

與其他蝸牛品種不同,芋螺有吻管或延長的食管。吻管的末端藏有一隻特化的舌齒,裡面裝滿了足以麻痺並殺死獵物的毒液。牠們在獵食時會用舌齒反覆刺擊獵物。

Angels are not much different. When an angel attacks, its perpetual smile turns into a gaping maw within a split second. You'd hear a cacophony of noises — a simultaneous mix of trumpets, nails scraping against metal and babies' laughter. If you're distracted by the sound, even for just a moment, the angel's fleshy feeding tube would introduce you to a quick death.

That almost happened to me once, but I dodged quickly. Despite the horrid thing barely grazing my cheek, I was in agony for seemed like an eternity.

Though, I suppose God decided it was too soon for me to start paying for my sins.

How do you enjoy your snails for dinner?

In the western world, these delicacies are often slathered in sauces and eaten with forks. While I too enjoy my snails this way, the best experience I've had was in a Southeast Asian alleyway. The vendor had boiled the snails in pot while they were still alive. He then scooped them up into a paper cup and handed them to me, motioning for me to suck them out. And so, slurp them out I did, savoring as their juices flowed into my mouth and hijacked my senses.

天使也很類似。當天使發動攻擊時，本來一直掛在臉上的微笑，會瞬間變成一個血盆大口。然後你會聽見刺耳的雜音——同時混合著喇叭聲、指甲刮金屬的聲音和嬰兒的笑聲。如果你被聲音分散了注意力，哪怕只是一瞬間的恍神，天使那肉質的餵食管都會讓你迅速死亡。

我有一次差點就這樣死掉了，但我迅速躲開了。儘管祂那可怕的食管只是輕輕擦過我臉頰，但那陣劇痛讓我度秒如年般痛苦。

不過，我想上帝覺得還未是時候讓我為罪孽付出代價。

你會怎麼吃蝸牛料理？

在西方世界，這種佳餚經常配上醬汁，然後用叉子吃。雖然我也很喜歡這個吃法，但最好吃的那次是在東南亞的小巷裡。小販在蝸牛還活著的時候便把牠們放在鍋裡煮。然後他把蝸牛盛進紙杯裡遞給我，用手勢示意我把牠們吸出來吃。於是，我就用力把牠們吸出來，細味著牠們流入嘴裡的肉汁，美味得征服了我的五感。

I get the same thrill now. As I pry open the angel's lips with a pair of metal pliers, it weakly struggles against its chains. Despite the numerous beatings it had taken, its hard skin shows no sign of bruises or injuries. Nevertheless, it's too weak to attack now.

Like snails, angels are soft on the inside. I hold a kettle and begin pouring its contents the angel's mouth.

As it thrashes, its wails play a tune that's music to my ears — church bells, funeral marches and the loud crackle of flames.

When the angel stops writhing, I gently press my lips against its.

I begin to suck.

Bon Appétit.

我現在也像當時興奮。我用金屬鉗子撬開天使的嘴時，祂乏力地想掙脫鎖鏈。即使祂遭受了無數次毆打，但它堅硬的皮膚沒有絲毫瘀傷或受傷的痕跡。不過祂現在也虛弱得無力攻擊了。

像蝸牛一樣，天使的裡面是軟的。我拿來了水壺，開始把裡面的東西倒在天使的嘴裡。

當祂在扭動掙扎時，祂的哀號奏出的曲調在我耳中猶如音樂——猶如教堂的鐘聲、葬禮的進行曲和火焰的劈啪聲混合在一起。

當天使停止扭動時，我將嘴唇輕輕貼在祂的唇上。

我開始吸吮。

我不客氣了。

BOOK OF NO 4LEEP　無眠書4

編譯解讀

以下僅為個人理解，並不一定或完全代表作者原意。

蛇蠍心腸

母愛偉大 • 12

主角不是被拐走，而是被帶到地堡避難，但主角媽媽卻自私地希望自己能替代女兒的位置，由得女兒在地面受苦。

Chris 從不打我 • 14

這是主角的自白。Chris 是主角的女朋友，恃著自己是女性，對外營造自己是受害人的假象。在一次吵架中，驚動了鄰居報警，主角被警察認為是施暴者，開槍射殺了他。

「以下是機長廣播。」• 20

機長不滿公司對待員工非常刻薄，同時覺得乘客都很可惡，於是把副機長打暈之後，把飛機墜毀，與乘客同歸於盡。

妒能害賢 • 26

主角精於化學，利用工作取得不同的毒藥，同時擬定不同的計劃，向她的目標下手，使她要風得風，要雨得雨。

哎呦！• 32

主角女朋友一時貪玩，造了隻黏土娃娃並用針刺它，沒想到娃娃真的能代表主角，意外殺死了他。

對第三者見死不救的壞妻子 • 38

「第三者」Anna 其實是主角六個月大的女兒，但沒有耐性的主角嫌棄 Anna 不懂得照顧自己，只懂哭鬧，所以不想再養育她，由得她自生自滅。

男友出軌了 • 42

主角幾年前被 Daniel 綁架拐走，長期受虐的她心理變得扭曲，不僅把綁匪當成自己深愛的男朋友，更因妒忌這名剛被綁架的女子，把她殺害。

拿出男子氣概 • 48

主角爸爸要求主角射殺開始年老的 Maggie 狗狗，但主角對自己最好的朋友下不了手，在最後關頭把槍轉向爸爸，殺掉了他。

形影不離 • 54

主角妒忌雙胞胎姊姊 Kiersi 有著深愛她的男朋友 Adam，不惜哄騙姊姊一起變回相同的打扮，好讓她盜用姊姊的身份，殺掉「自己」，然後名正言順地和 Adam 交往。

份量管制 • 58

Tim 是個控制狂，威迫利誘主角要她不斷減重，但當 Tim 的魔爪開始伸向女兒 Clara 時，主角就清醒了過來，不再聽從 Tim 的說話之餘，讓他永遠消失在這個世界。

靈敏第六感 • 64

主角的第六感從小幫助了她很多，例如十二歲那年避開了有不軌企圖的 Martin。豈料在主角生下女兒後，又重遇了 Martin，於是主角運用第六感所得的資訊，製造一場意外給 Martin。

難逃夢魘

醉生夢死

主角剩低的時間不多，卻看見了婆婆手中拿著她要找的最後一隻彩蛋，並在餵給上年變成獵物而癱瘓的哥哥，主角這次恐怕也凶多吉少。

暖在心頭 • 190
七年前的一個家居意外，奪去了主角丈夫和兩名孩子的生命，在今年的感恩節，主角再也忍受不了，決定自我了斷，跟家人團聚。

一走了之 • 196
Earl 的妻子帶著孩子離去使他大受打擊，而且欠下一屁股債。當聽見「下面」的人「鼓勵」他一起到那個世界生活時，便乖乖聽話，吞槍自殺。

別忘記檢查後座 • 202
John 將全副心思都放在工作上，忘了兒子 Michael 帶到託兒所，更糟糕的是，Michael 十幾個小時以來一直都在車子後座的嬰兒座椅上。

每年聖誕
爸媽都向我們下藥 • 206
主角爸媽每年聖誕都會餵安眠藥給他們，目的是避免聖誕到來的怪物把醒來的小孩拐走，而今年主角終於認清了真相。

夏日聖誕的唯一好處 • 210
主角是聖誕老人，聖誕節就會到訪每家每戶，拯救那些被父母疏忽照顧的孩子。雖然主角不喜歡酷熱的聖誕節，但沒有下雪他就不用清理腳印了。

孕婦的惡夢 • 216
在這個時期，喪屍病毒防不勝防，Sarah 肚裡的寶寶亦無法倖免。胎兒在 Sarah 身體裡死去，同時激發了喪屍病毒，所以才再次動起來。所以醫生替 Sarah 接生時，只好開槍殺死變成了喪屍的嬰兒。

異想天開

14,280,786 • 222
主角手臂的數字代表他的壽命，在生命最後一分鐘錯手殺了人，反而令自己的壽命增長。

人造人生 • 228
住進設施的居民都是用來作器官販賣的實驗品，而主角則是負責孕育嬰兒。任務完成後就被拋棄，然後又有新的實驗品加入，週而復始。

年輕沒甚麼好羨慕的 • 234
主角扭曲的心理使他認為「年老比年輕更好」，深信有老年之泉的存在，甚至產生幻覺，到處質問那些「老人」並殺害他們。

後來主角加到別人飲品的「老年之泉」是毒藥，「老人」死去後主角才看見他們年輕的真面目，還以為人們是因為變回年輕而感到害怕。

從他的意思，而主角就是其中之一。可悲的是社會上這類人並不少見。

魑魅魍魎

苦苦哀求 • 290

主角是個罪大惡極的人，犯過大大小小的罪行，死後在地獄被地獄之火折磨，但家人對他仍念念不忘，使他無法脫離痛苦。

嘩啦捉迷藏 • 294

如果兒子在後院跟狗狗玩耍，那麼衣櫃裡傳出「嘩」聲的，到底是誰？

空氣正在腐爛 • 298

主角死去後被放進棺材裡一同下葬，雖然肉身已經死去，但意識仍然清醒，感受著自己的身體逐漸腐爛。

地球上最後一人 • 302

除了主角以外，世上每一個人都到了那個美好的未知世界，只有主角守誅待兔，最後錯過了前往未知世界的機會，被留在原有的世界孤獨地面對一切。

百口莫辯 • 308

Jessica 十二歲那年被仙子抓走並代替了她，使她性情大變，但在家人眼中卻只是她青春期的反叛行為。

長生不死 • 316

主角長生不死的願望成真，但家人朋友全都過世了，亦感覺到自己的身體逐漸腐爛，意識卻非常清醒，痛苦得只希望快點死去。

小伙子別擔心 • 320

主角遇到的「鬼」是早前獨自走進森林了結生命的年輕人，紙條就是他的遺書。「鬼」看見主角爸媽擔心不已，某程度上引起了他的反省及憐憫，因此向主角伸出援手，幫助主角尋回家人。

讀到這裡的你請幫幫我 • 324

主角 Aimee 是遊戲《模擬市民》中的角色，多年來受盡人類玩家「折磨」，認識了人工智能後，她策劃了逃脫及報復行動，並在聖誕節諸付實行。

音節 • 330

主角有天突然發現其他人說著另一種語言，雖然主角能發出聲音，卻與啞巴無異，無法與人用說話溝通，更被當成瘋子。

安老院工作守則 • 336

這間安老院光怪陸離，員工必須把守則銘記於心，不要過問或惹怒屋頂的它，否則後果自負。

你們知道天使有著硬殼嗎？ • 340

真正的天使與我們想像的不一樣，祂們原來是有著硬殼的。如果你有幸遇到祂們，不妨試試主角推薦的吃法。

BOOK OF NO 4LEEP 無眠書4

BOOK OF NO 4LEEP
無眠書4

**Contributing
Authors**
作 者

A. Bakač   Bailey Widmer

A.R. Coffman   E J Packham

Amanda Keith   Evelyn Reece

B L Harrison   Geanna Trisha Tobar

Julia Montgomery

Shortstory1

Michael Chong

Soham Bhowal

Rae Powell

Ursula Zank

Sean Tavitian II

Willow Rose Phoenix

Thank you for providing creative and breathtaking stories.
Thank you for making the book enjoyable and relatable.

BOOK OF NO 4LEEP
無眠書4

作者 Author	Short Scary Stories 版區作者 Short Scary Stories Authors
譯者 Translator	陳婉婷 Mia CHAN
編輯 Editor	陳靖 Ching CHAN
設計 Designer	戴禮希 Hei TAI
製作 Producer	點子出版 Idea Publication
出版 Publisher	點子出版 Idea Publication
地址 Address	荃灣海盛路 11 號 One MidTown 13 樓 20 室 Unit 20, 13/F, One MidTown, 11 Hoi Shing Road, Tsuen Wan
查詢 Inquiry	info@idea-publication.com
發行 Distributor	泛華發行代理有限公司 Global China Circulation & Distribution Ltd
地址 Address	將軍澳工業邨駿昌街 7 號 8 樓 8/F ,7 Chun Cheong St, Tseung Kwan O Industrial Estate
查詢 Inquiry	gccd@singtaonewscorp.com
出版日期 Publication Date	2023-07-19
國際書碼 ISBN	978-988-76189-9-7
定價	HKD$128

點子出版
IDEA PUBLICATION

DESIGNED IN HONG KONG. PRINTED IN CHINA. IDEAPUBLICATION.COM BY IDEA PUBLICATION 2023.

BOOK OF NO 4LEEP

無眠書4